M000019245

Between Milk and India

Pia L. Bertucci

Copyright © 2015 Pia L. Bertucci

All rights reserved.

ISBN-10: 0692530711
ISBN-13: 978-0692530719
(Sorrento Books)

FOR MARK,
WITH ALL MY LOVE

CONTENTS

ACKNOWLEDGMENTS

My career as an academic, and my vocation as a writer, are due in no small part to the loving support, unwavering encouragement, and high-caliber, lifelong tutelage from my parents, Bruno F. and Beatrice J. Bertucci.
Da voi, tutto.

1

Tressa Novak finally boarded the 9:40 a.m. flight from the Raleigh Durham International Airport to Boston Logan at 11:00 a.m. after having waited with a lobby full of passengers for the weather delay to be lifted. It was the last week of December, and a cool, overcast morning in Raleigh, but everyone on the East Coast was already bracing for the possibility of an overdue winter storm. As the control tower, pilots and ground crews covered all their data and made their determinations, passengers speculated as to whether they would be leaving today, or would need to make other arrangements.

Sitting next to Tressa was a corpulent man in a somewhat threadbare, blue oxford shirt and baggy khakis, sweating profusely and reeking of a very stale tobacco odor, as though a lifetime of smoking had replaced most of his blood with nicotine. He was saying to no one, or to anyone who would listen (possibly to Tressa, although she had made a point of plugging herself into her Walkman so she would give off a definite signal of being unavailable), that this spate of unusual weather was in keeping with the upcoming millennium, or Y2K, which he uttered repeatedly. For this reason, the man continued, he had scheduled his return flight for after the second of January so he would not get caught in some kind of millennial time warp.

Over the past few months, as 1999 was drawing to a close, Tressa had conditioned herself to tune out whenever anyone brought up this millennium nonsense. *Who cares if the computers crashed once the year clicked over to 2000?* She was old enough to remember life without computers, or at least when they were still considered rare and exotic instruments. She was also one of the few free-lance writers who wrote out her magazine and journal articles by hand, or dictated them into her micro tape recorder, before she entered them on her home computer.

Tressa did have to admit that when it came to doing research for these articles, the advance of the internet search engines made working from home infinitely easier. Still, she often found herself feeling nostalgic for the immediacy of the old devices. There was something about being able to manipulate typewriters, record players, or even the old microfilm machines directly with your hands and knowing instantly the result that you could expect. If you lifted the needle on a record, you could place it on the exact part of the song you wanted to hear without having to worry about the player sticking or freezing the way CD players often did. Of course, records did scratch, but she had never needed to throw out her record player. For almost two decades, she had owned the same Panasonic, and would simply buy new records if the old ones became too scratched. Conversely, she had now been through eight different CD players in her adult life. As for typewriters, there was something special about the oily smell of the ribbon and the pressure you had to exert on each key to form a letter. The care you had to take to organize your thoughts beforehand, to write clearly and spell correctly bolstered the feeling that you were really working at something. It made you that much more vigilant; you made extra copies and stored them in different places. With her new reliance on computers, Tressa had become careless and had often lost entire documents when she had been working through a stream of consciousness and forgot to save the thing as she went along. So if a technological meltdown was looming, she concluded, so be it.

As for a more drastic Armageddon-like outcome to the advent of the year 2000 predicted by some soothsayers, this did not faze Tressa in the least. A few months earlier, she had seen the end-of-the-world film *Deep Impact* and found it oddly comforting. She recognized this might not be a healthy sign, but the way things had been going lately in her life – a downward, turbulent spiral to say the least – she sometimes felt that if the whole world came to a crashing halt it would be somewhat of a relief to her.

Tressa was on her way to visit her aunt Regina. It was Regina's sixtieth birthday and Tressa was quite sure the poor woman would be all alone otherwise. Regina was her father's younger sister and had very little to do with the otherwise tightly knit extended family.

I've been excommunicated,

Regina had lamented to Tressa on an earlier visit. This was somewhat of an exaggeration. In fact, Tressa noticed that the estrangement, stemming from one of those misunderstandings between loved ones that can only be blown out of proportion when there are such deep emotional ties and so much history, did not seem to weigh too heavily on her rather eccentric aunt. In another era, Regina Novak would have been classified as a "spinster." Now, in the enlightened era of the nineties, Tressa's sister and cousins referred to Aunt Regina as a "crazy cat lady." Tressa acknowledged there was more than a grain of truth behind this moniker. She never completely managed to remove the different colored hairs from Regina's three cats from her clothing after one of these visits, despite multiple washings and several rolls of lint brush inserts. However, the fact that her aunt lived alone with her cats did not make the old woman unpleasant to spend time with. Regina herself was fastidious in her appearance, and seemed satisfied with her career as an audio book narrator, or *actor*, to use her term. It was a job she had done for ages, initially begun to fill in the gaps when she could not find work as a *real actor*. At some point Regina had adopted it as a permanent profession when it was clear those roles had stopped coming altogether. Undoubtedly, she would continue to do book narrations as long as the work kept coming.

Regina had never married, but had certainly had her string of involvements. The most recent, with an aging radio DJ named Peter, had lasted for close to ten years, a record for Regina, but had ended tragically six years ago when Peter's somewhat pickled liver finally gave out on him. Imbibing was a pastime in which

Regina and Peter had equally over-indulged. In fact, Regina blamed her solitude of the past few years not on her age, but on the fact that most men in their advanced years were teetotalers for health reasons.

Regina's drinking was perhaps the only challenging aspect of Tressa's visit with her favorite relative. Regina was neither an aggressive nor a sloppy drunk, but as she aged she did become more forgetful, often leaving appliances on, doors unlocked, or windows open. Then there was the time that Regina herself lost her key and went to stay with a friend without remembering that she had a houseguest who would be showing up. Regina's daily dosing of gin and tonics did not improve her memory function. Despite her aunt's unpredictable behavior, however, Tressa enjoyed the curious balance between true familial affection and breathing room that Regina provided on these visits.

Indeed, this particular visit was not solely motivated by Tressa's concern for her aunt. Although Tressa did appreciate Regina's perspective and encouragement, she also needed some time and room to sort out her life, a life that had been going along just fine until it blew up one day without any warning. *Well*, Tressa imagined Regina's sage words gently chiding her, *there had been some warnings*. Tressa had just chosen not to see them.

When exactly did it all go to Hell exactly? Tressa and Daniel had been married for almost twenty years. They were both young when they married: Tressa had just turned twenty, and Daniel was twenty-two. It had been a decision essentially motivated by the fact that Tressa was three-months pregnant by this time. They had only been dating for a few weeks when Tressa became aware of her condition. Daniel had recently decided to join the Air Force. When Tressa found out she was pregnant, she contemplated not even telling Daniel. She was just not convinced she could see a future with him. She toyed with the idea of just letting him enlist and disappear to some remote corner of the globe while she slipped off and raised the child alone as a single parent. Somehow, however, her pregnancy hormones got the best of her and she broke down and told him. By that point, she had lost her nerve, and was convinced that she could not go through it alone. As soon as Daniel found out, he pulled the plug on his enlistment plans and decided to take a job, any job, near home so that he and Tressa could be together.

Two years after their son Ellis was born, they had a daughter, Kassie. Over the next few years, Tressa worked as a teller at a bank and went to school at night. Daniel and her mom filled in the gaps with childcare. Eventually, Daniel landed a plum job at a large international firm overseeing all of their security. Tressa went on to earn a Master's in Accounting and became a CPA for a prominent bank. By the time Ellis started middle school, Tressa and Daniel had overcome a series of emotional and financial ups and downs, and now owned a nice suburban home. All was well. Or, so it would seem.

At some point, Tressa felt overcome by a heaviness she could not shake. She and Daniel were living almost parallel lives, coming together only occasionally out of either physical or functional necessity. At least, Tressa would console herself, Ellis and Kassie seemed to be untouched by their parents' developing estrangement. In fact, they were thriving. Besides being model students, her children were busy with friends, part-time jobs, and extracurricular activities. When Tressa watched so many of her colleagues and friends teetering on the edge of insanity as their teens plunged into everything from drugs, drunk driving and various misdemeanors, she felt blessed by comparison.

Then, just when she thought she was out of the woods, it happened. When Ellis's High School graduation was behind him and his first semester at UNC Greensboro was only three weeks away, her sweet boy, her baby who had clung to her in his childhood, who had always been so close to her, and told her everything, was suddenly overtaken by an unrecognizable alien being.

When did it start? Tressa was not sure, having surely ignored all the signs, Ellis having retreated inward months earlier, keeping to himself, no longer talking her ear off at every opportunity. For her, the pivotal moment occurred one rainy Saturday morning, a morning as grey, dark and hopeless as the previous night had been full of light, hope, and renewed purpose.

That Friday she had found herself embarking on a path that she had previously vowed she would never travel: she had accepted a dinner invitation from a male friend of hers and her husband, Federico Suarez, better known as Rico. He was married to one of Daniel's colleagues, a statuesque, platinum blonde who went by the fittingly ostentatious nickname of Kiki (her real name was Charlotte.) The two couples had been friends for years. It was not unusual for the four of them to get together socially, as a group, but Tressa had no illusions when she accepted this solitary invitation from Rico; she knew that suddenly and inexplicably the rules of the game had changed. Oddly enough, she mused now, she had taken it in stride, as though Rico's proposition had been nothing more than trying out a new gym after work or changing hair stylists.

As she lay in bed that Friday night, alone – Daniel was still out at a cigar bar with work friends – Tressa recalled all that had transpired between her and Rico, what they had said, had done, and had contemplated doing. There had been kisses, embraces and promises exchanged, but nothing beyond that. Overall, she could not land on how she felt. Guilty? Happy? The only thing she was sure of was the conflict brewing inside her. That sudden and unexpected, even long forgotten feeling of just being alive again had made her aware of the sleepwalker state she had been in for so long. After that evening, she knew she could no longer suppress what had been going on in her marriage. However, she would never have a chance to sort out those feelings in a deliberate or thoughtful way.

The following morning, that fateful Saturday, she woke up to a stream of audible profanity emanating from Ellis's room. It was not Ellis, but Daniel who summoned her in there.

Tressa made her way down the hallway, somewhat shaky without her morning coffee, fighting her already growing hostility at the fact that she had been deprived of one of her few precious "sleep-in" days. Later, she would reflect that no amount of coffee could have prepared her for what came next.

Ellis was not there, having decided to sleep over at a friend's house the night before. Daniel, who had an 8:30 a.m. tee time that morning, had gone into Ellis's empty room to look for some golf balls and had stumbled upon a veritable addict's den in his son's closet.

By the time Tressa reached her husband, he was pulling out empty vodka bottles, strange looking pipes and lighters, and various other paraphernalia for which Tressa had no frame of reference, and strewing them around the room as he threw them over his shoulder.

"Can you believe this shit?"

Tressa had never seen Daniel like this. Throughout their courtship and marriage, he had his moments of passion and excitability, and had always seemed to possess a repressed rage that instead found its outlet in destructive comments and sarcastic jokes at others' expense. However, never did he let it all go as he did in that moment.

The days and sleepless nights that followed blended into what at the time felt like a lifetime of interminable suffering. They put UNC Greensboro on hold. Daniel and Tressa checked Ellis into rehab, and after he was released, they found him a therapist to help sort out the root of this downward spiral. If they were hoping for resolution or for answers, they never found them. Since Ellis had already turned eighteen by this time, his parents were no longer allowed access to his medical records unless Ellis signed a release, and he firmly and steadfastly refused to do so. The attending physician put Ellis on a few medications to combat his diagnosed depression and arranged for him to meet with a therapist on a weekly basis. Daniel and Tressa would later learn, from the bills that they received, that Ellis attended exactly two of those therapy sessions. The last session took place approximately five days before Ellis disappeared, seemingly, off the face of the earth.

An audible burst of static pierced the non-distinct din of the airport waiting area, followed by the flight attendant's measured speech with predictable cadence informing the passengers that it was finally time to board. When the attendant announced the pre-boarding of parents with small children, Tressa felt a nostalgic pang. She had to laugh at herself; she had certainly flown innumerable times over the many years since her children had been small. Somehow, however, the pain and tenderness of her open wound smarted at the reminder that not only was she a parent to two children who were almost adults, but that one of them was gone completely from her life, possibly forever.

Once on the plane, Tressa settled into her coveted window seat and proceeded to pull down the shade; it was the relative reclusiveness the window seat provided, and not the view, that made it essential for her when traveling. She pulled out her Sport Walkman cassette player and put in a tape of Talk Talk. A few years earlier, she had won the Walkman in a raffle at work. At the time, she had no use for such a thing so she gave it to Ellis who was initially excited about it, until a few months afterwards, that Christmas, when he asked for a CD Walkman and gave her back the antiquated model. It sat in her top dresser drawer, until some time after that Tuesday in November when Ellis disappeared.

It had been an ordinary, otherwise uneventful Tuesday. Tressa and Daniel had gone to work like any other weekday. Kassie had gone to school, and Ellis had slept in. For the past several weeks, Ellis had been working occasional shifts at the Food Lion grocery store near their house, and had decided that he would start taking classes at Wake Technical College that summer. Slowly, but surely, Tressa thought her son was shaking off the lethargy and depression that had overtaken him just a few months ago. She no longer hesitated as she stood on the doorstep of their house at the end of a long day; the once all-too vivid fear of finding an unresponsive Ellis inside had started to ebb. In the mornings, Ellis would take walks with their dog, Cocoa, and in the evenings, he would occasionally watch old films with her, or sports with Daniel. Ellis was not exactly back to his old self; he no longer hung out in the garage with Daniel and tinkered on cars, nor did he go out with his friends, but at least he seemed to be regaining control and a certain degree of optimism in his life. Daniel, however, found Ellis's situation progressively frustrating, and Tressa had to beg, bargain and even hold out ultimata to keep him from coming down too hard on their son. Daniel thought Ellis had it "too good" or "too soft" and would only continue to languish as long as Tressa "enabled" this inertia. Tressa, however, believed with every fiber of her being that Ellis was consistently a heartbeat away from snapping, from giving up, from ending it all in the most horrific and tragic way; a way that was still too abstract to imagine. She was not willing to gamble when the stakes were so high, nor would she allow Daniel to do so.

On that Tuesday as she stood on the doorstep fishing her key out of her cluttered handbag, Tressa experienced a resurgence of the old fears; that soul-shattering feeling of dread that some unimaginable terror lay behind the beveled glass windows of the entryway. She sensed that once she opened that door, her life would change forever. She would never be whole again.

Tressa raced upstairs to find that this time the premonition came true. Unlike her waking nightmares had threatened, there were no pills, rope, or blood. Instead, once inside Ellis's room, Tressa found only emptiness and silence. There was no note. Ellis's belongings had been cleared out; not entirely, but his closet was bare enough for Tressa to realize, unequivocally, that he was gone.

In the following days that dissolved into weeks, Tressa and Daniel exhausted every imaginable civil resource: local police, FBI, internet postings and posters in local businesses. Finally, they took out a second mortgage on their house to hire a private detective who traipsed across the country and was only able to uncover one dead-end lead through DMV records, specifically a transfer of title, in Henderson, Nevada. The private detective was able to determine that Ellis had sold his car to an elderly man, an old widower named John Harris, well known to all the locals as simply, "Harris." Harris told the private detective that Ellis had been driving around town with a "For Sale" sign in his car window. Harris called the phone number listed on the sign and met Ellis that same day. According to Harris, Ellis was in a bit of a hurry to close the sale, claiming that he was upgrading to a newer model and needed the money to use as a down payment. Harris paid him in cash. The private detective and local officials in Nevada ran Ellis's name through various financial circuits, but could find no records of any credit card or bank transactions in Ellis's name.

Looking back on it now, Tressa realized that this was the moment when everything changed forever. She and Daniel had been plunged into a bottomless abyss.

Daniel's initial emotional reaction to the lead in Nevada was anger, which he voiced bitterly. He was furious that their son had sold the car, a vintage 1975 BMW 2500 in mint condition. He and Ellis had worked on it laboriously, but joyfully, overhauling and polishing it off with a new engine and a multitude of other new parts. Ellis "cashing in the car," as Daniel put it, was an unforgivable offense in his eyes. After that revelation, whenever Tressa mentioned Ellis's name, Daniel would launch another one of his venomous invectives against their son. Tressa was stunned. She begged and pleaded with her husband – sometimes sobbing, sometimes screaming, and sometimes icily calm – to follow up on this precious lead. They could not stop now; they had to press on until they found Ellis. However, Daniel would not budge. Up until that point, the couple had been united in their grief, but with this aggressive shift in Daniel's attitude, Tressa realized she was now irretrievably alone. Daniel closed his account with the private detective and went back to his daily routine, as stony and silent as ever. Three nights into this staged return to normalcy in their household, Tressa coaxed her superiors at the bank into spontaneously releasing her accumulated vacation time without any advance warning. She flew to Nevada alone, renting a car and driving through three states with boxes of posters that featured a smiling Ellis in his prom tuxedo and a string of contact phone numbers, with the chilling caption:

Have you seen me?

Tressa hit as many points as she could manage from Las Vegas to Taos, New Mexico, focusing on locales she thought her son might be inclined to frequent. In the meantime, she hired her own private detective and sent him to California and Mexico to chase a few more dead-end leads.

Her resources virtually dried up, and with no more information than before she began her journey, Tressa finally returned home. Tressa's vacation time was converted into an indefinite leave of absence, which was eventually followed by a letter from the President of the bank. Tressa had ignored the many calls from her immediate supervisors, as well as the eventual letter that informed her that she no longer had a position. Time stood still, or, ceased to have meaning. Christmas and New Year's Day came and went with only a semblance of festivity. There was a tree, there were gifts, including some for Ellis that both she and Kassie had wrapped and left under the tree. They felt a bit like sacrificial offerings.

By mid-January, Tressa's last fibers of hope unraveled. She holed up in her study, barely leaving her futon. A little voice nagged at her, reminding her that she still had one child who needed her, but Tressa could barely find the energy to get out of bed.

After countless days of lying trapped in a black hole of despair, Tressa's sister Liza came to stay with her. Liza's presence became a sliver of sunlight through the previously drawn heavy drapes. Liza had a way of unobtrusively taking control, sorting through bills and various household affairs, making sure Kassie had everything she needed including dinners for the week that she stored in the deep freeze. Daniel appreciated this as well, but Liza's efforts did nothing to quell his growing resentment. Because of this, Tressa had not bothered to share with Daniel the troubling information she had uncovered about Ellis on her Western Odyssey that left innumerable unanswered questions.

Tressa had found signs that her son had been gambling, as well as a string of shady acquaintances along the way. They were young people who looked like poster children for the grunge revolution. Several of them knew Ellis, recognized his picture, but had no clue where he had ended up after his transitory stopover in that particular quarter. What Tressa found even more troubling was that the few people she did manage to locate who knew her son did not seem to show the slightest interest in his well-being.

Among the many jobs Ellis had apparently held included a busboy at a rundown bistro in Santa Fe, a cashier and handyman at a counter-culture henna and tattoo parlor in Reno, a gopher for a sleazy attorney who had him serve papers on deadbeat dads and cheating spouses, and a bagger at a Safeway outside of San Francisco.

Ellis had always had a charismatic and winning way with people; an ease that she had always envied. Tressa would often laugh in spite of herself in tense social situations, especially obligatory business shindigs, as she would often imagine how her young son could slide into any crowd of strangers and almost instantly make them as comfortable with him as he seemed to be with them. Despite his charm, good looks, intelligence and inherent goodness – the last being a point Daniel would now call into question – it now seemed that there had been no one in his new life who was there for him, who even seemed to give a damn.

To imagine her child, alone and vulnerable in the world, and possibly suffering, filled Tressa with excruciating and unending pain. Tressa spent most of her time sifting through old pictures and running memories through her mind constantly. All she could see, both in the tangible Kodak images and her mental slideshow, was a happy, smiling, child who embraced life and wanted to experience as much as he could. Ellis had excelled in virtually every sport offered through the schools and neighborhood recreation centers, had taken a post on the High School newspaper, and had even volunteered with a church youth group at local food banks. There was photo after photo of Ellis on hockey skates, holding a lacrosse pole, poised for a backward flip into the lake, hamming it up with his buddies on the soccer field. Tressa winced at the perfect beauty of her son's effortless and genuine smile, his thick golden mane windswept on a family sailing expedition, or, the toddler Ellis on a hot summer day curled up in Tressa's lap.

In so many ways, he had always seemed to be perfect. There had been times that predated Ellis's actual disappearance, when Tressa, feeling more vulnerable than usual, would allow her mind to wander to the most unimaginable *what ifs*.

His affable demeanor, his good nature, his genuine desire to help and be decent to people led Tressa to conclude that Ellis was *too good for this life*.

Throughout his youth, she could all too easily imagine Ellis being taken away from her, although she would never go so far as to fill in the details of the tragedy in these day mares. Instead, her mind would leap to her delivering his eulogy, barely choking out the beautifully and tragically fitting words of A.E. Houseman in *To an Athlete Dying Young*.

How and when had her son lost his way? Unlike her daughter Kassie who wore her heart on her sleeve, Ellis had always held his emotions close to his chest, and rarely revealed what he was thinking or how he was feeling. Tressa and Daniel had only met a handful of their son's good friends from high school, and had never met a single girlfriend. Was it something there? It had only recently begun to dawn on Tressa how vast Ellis's secret world may have been. Had he experienced a traumatic relationship setback? Was it a question of sexual orientation? Had he been afraid to face his own parents? Would she have been able to handle that? Certainly. Would Daniel? She thought so, but could not be entirely sure. And then, there was the question of the drugs and alcohol. Was Ellis self-medicating to overcome some great emotional or psychic crisis in his life? Was there something else more dark and sinister lurking in the shadows to which she, his own mother, had been oblivious? Or, had Ellis just dabbled in substance experimentation like many teens, but then found himself at the mercy of those demons? What bothered her most was the fear that she might never know.

At Liza's urging, Tressa started running again and spent her other free hours writing what started as journal entries; a cathartic exercise to help her unpack all of the conflicting emotions Ellis's disappearance had created.

By now, Tressa was leaving the house and braving the outside world again, attending her daughter's swim meets, or just shopping with Liza and Kassie. Occasionally, Tressa would set herself up at a café with outdoor seating and compose reams of entries in her notebooks. Initially Tressa intended to keep these compositions relatively secret, sharing them only with Liza. However, at some point her writing took on a life of its own and morphed into general musings about the youth of today and family life. Liza was convinced that Tressa's elegant style and keen, albeit melancholic, insight might catch the eye of a family or women's magazine editor. After blindly sending out a few writing samples, Liza landed Tressa a few gigs with local papers and free community publications. Within two months, Tressa's columns caught the eye of a nationally syndicated paper and before long, she was able to piece together enough work between that column and a few women's magazines to begin to pull her family out of their current financial quagmire.

A year had passed; another Christmas had come and gone, with more wrapped offerings for Ellis under the tree, much to Daniel's annoyance. Tressa and Daniel, though still married and living in the same house, had virtually no contact anymore, even going as far as trading off attendance at their daughter's extracurricular activities. Kassie seemed to be coping in spite of it all, venting only occasionally to Tressa about how much she really missed and worried about her brother, and how truly dysfunctional their family had become. There was one thing in particular that Kassie said to Tressa that had finally pushed her to shake off the last vestiges of murky passivity and inaction:

"What are you and Dad doing anyway? Do you think it is somehow better for any of us that there is so much silence and unhappiness in this house? Come on! This is no life. You are not living. You can't put the rest of your life on hold while we wait for Ellis to come back. Do it for me, if not for yourself, Mom!"

Tressa felt humbled by this harsh reality check dealt by her own teenage daughter, but she was also thoroughly impressed by Kassie's insight and sense of self. Tressa decided she needed to get away for a few days to clear her head, a decision that Kassie supported, and to which Daniel did not object.

The shrill ding alerting passengers that they could unfasten their seatbelts and move about the cabin woke Tressa from her musings. Tressa had no intention to stir until they landed at Logan. She pressed 'play' on her Walkman, closed her eyes and let the melancholy strains of Talk Talk's "Happiness is Easy" wash over her.

The landing was a bit bumpy. Otherwise, Tressa might not have woken so easily. She had fallen into the deepest of sleeps, as though at home she was always on guard, sleeping like the proverbial dog with one eye always open, ready to launch into action if need be. Had she dreamt? They say you always dream, but you do not always remember your dreams. These days Tressa wished she could be more aware of her dreams. Did Ellis appear to her as she navigated that ethereal terrain? If she could remember those dreams, would he have left her some clues? Did they lie hidden in her unconscious mind? Tressa was so engrossed in these thoughts, that she almost did not notice the elderly woman in colorful, flowing rayon fabrics running up to her in the baggage claim area, until they were almost face-to-face.

It had not been that long since she had last seen her, but Tressa was struck by how much her aunt had aged. Tressa threw her arms around Regina, and refused her stoic aunt's offer to heft her heavy bag. As they hustled out of the airport in search of a cab, Regina talked almost as briskly as she walked, and Tressa found she had to double her pace to keep up with her aged aunt. Regina hailed a cab with an elegant and confident gesture. Tressa and Regina settled into the cab and waited for the reassuring thud of the trunk. Within seconds, they were speeding off towards downtown. Regina had made lunch reservations at a *fantastic new place* she just was dying to show her niece. All of Tressa's previous visits had started this way, with a certain frenzy and over-the-top ceremony.

The fantastic new place was actually an Irish pub which made Tressa wonder how much of her aunt's mind had been corroded by her passion for the drink. However, once she experienced the surprisingly delectable sensation of fresh corned beef on rye accompanied by a mushroom and potato soup and paired with a Guinness, she had to give her aunt credit for her good taste. As was often the routine on these visits, Regina uttered her usual disclaimer that there was no set agenda for Tressa's stay, however, she did have a few things in mind. Regina proceeded to tell Tressa about a friend, an oboe player in the symphony, who had given her two tickets for that night at the Boston Opera House. The following night they had third row seats for a rock opera that had made the rounds in London and Broadway and was now playing the Colonial Theater. The rest of their calendar was open.

"So how are you holding up, girlie?"

This was Regina's way of showing concern and affection, and Tressa was happy that the silence over Ellis's disappearance had been broken. She wondered how other people dealt with their grief. Tressa imagined that there must be a great many people who lock themselves in their denial and keep their misery tamped down at all costs. Tressa had initially found it somewhat soothing to talk to Daniel, until their son's name and existence became unmentionable concepts in their household. She had talked to Liza at length, until she stopped herself one day. After weeks of self-reproach, as well as anger at herself, at Daniel, and at the world, she could hear how she sounded, and more importantly, what she had become: hopeless, bitter and trapped in a masochistic vortex that was draining her energy and, she was quite certain, making her sister just a bit weary of hearing it all.

Talking to Regina, however, was defensible since they had only spoken briefly on the phone a few times since Ellis's disappearance. Tressa started to navigate that all-too-well traveled path of this narrative as she related the first signs of Ellis's troubles and the deafening silence in his empty room, the Tuesday he disappeared. Somewhere, in the middle of her summation of her journey to Las

Vegas and beyond, Tressa stopped her story. Now, instead of hearing her own voice as the lament of the hopeless and burdensome victim, Tressa heard the colorless echo of a tale told so often it had been stripped of its weight and its soul. It was not that Tressa had stopped feeling that pain, but she herself had grown tired of trying to put into words things that still had no discernible shape or intelligible meaning.

"Essentially, Aunt Regina, I've hit rock bottom and I don't know where to go from here."

Regina smiled sympathetically, but did not push Tressa to continue beyond her conclusion. They finished the rest of their lunch with only superficial banter about family gossip, news of Tressa's latest columns, and Regina's latest audio book project that she would finish recording within the next two days. She enthusiastically informed Tressa that it was by far her favorite, *If on a Winter's Night a Traveler...* by Italo Calvino, translated into English. When Tressa did not reveal any spark of recognition of the author or the tale, Regina slammed both of her hands down on the sturdy oak table and said with her usual theatrical flair,

"You haven't lived... No. You haven't *experienced* literature in all of its transformative power until you read this book."

They finished their lunch and Tressa snuck her credit card to the waiter to forestall her aunt's insistence on paying. Regina rolled her eyes and groaned in dramatic protest when she caught sight of Tressa signing the receipt. Immediately after thanking her, Regina grabbed her niece's hand just as she had when Tressa was a little girl, and pulled her out of the pub. Tressa followed her aunt obediently into a bookstore a few doors down. The bookstore doubled as an internet café, and Tressa fought the urge to check her email since she knew her aunt still did not own a computer. This would have certainly been an affront, so Tressa made a mental note to come back another time and waited beside her aunt at the counter. Regina had just asked the upper middle-aged man sporting a long ponytail and a black leather vest if they had Calvino's book in stock.

"Aunt Regina, can't I just borrow your copy when you're done?"

Tressa asked quietly, primarily to diffuse the fuss she felt her aunt was making over her, but Regina would not hear of it.

"Tressa my girl, I have come to appreciate in my wise dotage that there are certain cardinal rules one must respect in order to maintain a sense of equilibrium and Zen. One of those things is *not* to lend out books. I would wager that more friendships and relationships have been impaired or severed through this all-too-common practice. You, the book owner, expect to receive the book back again one day, but chances are, the borrower, even if he or she has the best of intentions, may forget. They may misplace it, or, worst-case scenario, loan it out to a third party who has even less regard for its original owner. If you, the book's owner, think you can avoid this awkward and aggravating experience by putting a bookplate in your book, you are even more gravely mistaken. All of the aforementioned conclusions can still play out, but now you know that the book is clearly branded, therefore, any failure of the borrower to return it is all the more unforgiveable."

Tressa was not sure whether she should laugh at the intensity with which Regina proposed this firm philosophy on book ownership, or marvel at her aunt's resolution. As it turned out, the man who Regina would later identify as the owner of the store interrupted this exchange with the announcement that he did not have the book in stock, but could order it.

However, he added, he would have to ask for a pre-payment. This was not exactly a book that was in demand, and if Regina did not claim it, he would be saddled with a book that few would find interesting. This made Regina furrow her brow, and for a moment, Tressa feared her aunt would unleash another soliloquy on the virtues of Calvino's landmark narrative. Instead, Regina rummaged in her oversized bag until she pulled out her wallet. Tressa motioned that she would pay, but Regina playfully slapped her hand away (playful in spirit, thought Tressa's hand would sting for the next few minutes).

"This is a gift. You wouldn't insult an old woman by refusing her gift, would you? Besides, I owe you any number of birthday and Christmas gifts..."

Regina placed the order and asked how long it would take for the book to arrive. The man announced that it was uncertain, but since a store in New York had a copy, he could have it as soon as that Friday, New Year's Eve. They would be open until 6:00 p.m. that day.

"Just in time!"

Regina announced gleefully, with a slap on the counter similar to the blow she had dealt the pub table. Tressa would be leaving that Saturday, on New Year's Day, and she promised Regina that she herself would come back to pick it up in case Regina was busy finishing her own project. Regina seemed satisfied with this arrangement and the two caught a cab back to Regina's apartment to rest until the symphony that night.

2

The next three days passed calmly, with a varied, but still somewhat predictable routine that involved Tressa treating Regina to a birthday dinner and movie, long walks, naps, more dinners out and various cultural activities. On Friday morning, Tressa woke to a terrible thunderstorm, which seemed so uncharacteristic for that time of year and that part of the country.

Usually, no matter how early Tressa awoke, Regina was already in the kitchen with a pot of coffee made, toast and eggs, or oatmeal and fruit laid out on the table. This morning, Tressa was surprised to find that she had slept in until 10:00. More surprising, the kitchen was empty and dark. She checked her watch again, and once she realized the unmistakable fact that it was midmorning and there was no sign of her aunt, nor a note saying she had run out for yogurt or orange juice as she had done on previous visits, Tressa succumbed instantly to a feeling of panic and dread. She shuffled to her aunt's room, and after she nearly tripped in the hallway, shed the fuzzy slippers she had borrowed. Making her way quickly across the cold hardwood floor she knocked tentatively on Regina's bedroom door.

When there was no answer, Tressa tried the door. When it opened, she went in and made her way to Regina's bed. The room did not have the feeling or the smell of death, although Tressa had not ever experienced death firsthand before. She had just always imagined that there would be unmistakable sensory markers in such a situation. It was too hot and dry, her aunt's old-fashioned radiator doing more than its job, and Tressa licked her lips and swallowed several times as though it would help her rehydrate. Once she had reached the bed, she stopped, unsure of how to proceed. She called out her aunt's name a few times, and got no response; although two of Regina's cats lifted their heads from the pillow they were sharing with their mistress and looked at Tressa expectantly. Tressa then employed a maneuver that was second nature to her, one that she had used frequently when Ellis and Kassie had been small. She placed her hand on her aunt's side, touching her abdomen below the ribcage to make sure she was breathing. Upon the touch of her niece's apparently icy hand, Regina bolted upright in bed and looked at Tressa with an air of confusion before she showed any sign of consciousness or recognition.

"I'm sorry, dear. I guess I was in a deep sleep."

"Are you feeling OK, Aunt Regina? You feel like you are burning up!"

"Yes. Actually, no. I don't feel right. But, not to worry, I think it is just a cold or transitory flu or something. Nothing I haven't experienced a thousand other times during this unpredictable weather. Be a dear and bring me a couple of aspirin and a large glass of water. I'm afraid I'll have to leave you to explore on your own today."

"Nonsense! I am not going to leave you like this. I can stay and get some writing done. Besides, the weather is unbearable out there. Freezing rain if you can believe it. I'll be right back with your aspirin. Anything else? Coffee? Orange Juice? Toast?"

Regina waved away Tressa's other suggestions, and upon receiving her aspirin, swallowed them with what appeared to be great difficulty, and washed them down with half the glass of water.

Tressa heard the phone ringing in the other room and offered to go and get it.

It was the quirky bookstore-café owner, who wanted to let them know that the Calvino book had arrived and that they could pick it up anytime.

She relayed this to her aunt who suggested Tressa go out immediately to get it. Regina promised that she would be fine, and that this was a good time to leave her alone since she needed to sleep anyway.

"And besides,"

She suggested,

"At least this way you'll have something decent to read. I'll inscribe it for you once you bring it back."

In the Novak family, a tradition had been passed down that everyone still followed, including Tressa's father and Tressa herself, in which the gift of a book had to be accompanied by a personalized inscription by the one who bestowed the gift. Tressa smiled at this thought and asked her aunt for directions to the store.

"The bookstore? It's between Milk and India."

Regina muttered this weakly with her eyes closed, and for a moment, Tressa was convinced that the fever had made her aunt delirious. Regina had fallen back asleep so Tressa went into her aunt's living room in search of a phone book. She could not remember the name of the store, but was sure she would recognize it if she saw it. Sure enough, it stood out instantly: "The Underground Traveler's Bookstore." She had meant to ask the owner the significance of the store's name the first time they had come in, but she had been distracted and swept away by her aunt's energy and frenetic pace. Tressa laughed when she saw the address of the bookstore listed in the yellow page ad: 173 Milk Street.

Once she arrived at the location, (she had hailed a cab since she did not want to wake her aunt for directions, and the weather was too horrid for exploring) she noticed the cross street, India. Regina's description had been purely geographical. *Between Milk and India.*

Tressa walked into the store and was unpleasantly surprised to discover only a negligible climatic change from the cold outside. She looked around and saw people oblivious to the near Arctic chill in the obviously old building as they huddled close to their coffee or tea, at the book and magazine racks, or at one of the pay-per-use computer stations *The Underground* provided. Tressa inhaled that intoxicating aroma of strong, brewed coffee and excitedly ordered herself a Vanilla Latte and asked to book an hour on one of the computers. Although Tressa did want to check for new writing jobs that were usually forwarded to her via email since she worked remotely, she was fully aware that her excitement stemmed from the possibility of an email from her friend Rico. After their one evening out together, over a year ago, and the disastrous, seemingly unrelated events of the next day concerning Ellis, Tressa had broken off all contact. Because their spouses worked together, however, Rico had learned about their recent family tragedy. During those first few weeks, Rico had sent Tressa emails and left her a few voicemails on her work phone expressing his empathy and concern for her son's disappearance. Tressa had responded half-heartedly to a couple of the emails, but had allowed their potential romantic story to evaporate as she was consumed by the ensuing months of grief and unanswered questions.

More than a year later, Tressa found that simply making the decision to take the trip to Boston had filled her with a renewed sense of purpose and a limited, but usable store of energy. She still was not sure what exactly had motivated her, but the day before her trip, she had spontaneously sent Rico an email. Ostensibly, to anyone who might have intercepted it, the message appeared to be innocuous enough. She thanked him for all his well wishes and apologized for her lack of communication. She closed with a seemingly friendly suggestion to meet sometime for coffee. Tressa was quite sure Rico would be able to read between the lines and glimpse an opening or a hint of an invitation to pick up where they had left off. She knew this and sent the message anyway. She had no regrets or feelings of compunction; she neither tried to convince herself that it meant nothing, nor did she rationalize that what she was doing was forgivable since her marriage was over. Instead, when Tressa sent that message to Rico, and as she anticipated his response, she was filled with an almost manic sense of joy. In some abstract but also almost palpable way, she realized that she had decided to reclaim her place among the living.

The woman behind the counter informed Tressa that there would be a twenty-minute wait for a computer, unless Tressa wanted to use the old Mac behind the magazine racks. The computer itself was fine, but the internet connections were sometimes spotty. Tressa did not want to wait in that cold store any longer than she needed to; she already felt the cold and damp from those few moments outside seeping into her body. In the end, she booked an hour on the old machine and took her coffee with her. The young woman handed her a small, square reservation pod with lights that Tressa had seen on a few occasions at restaurants when awaiting a table, and promised that Tressa would be notified if a better computer opened up.

Tressa tossed the pod into her purse and headed towards the old computer, which was in an alcove next to the bathrooms. Once she got there, Tressa cursed herself as she remembered her original purpose for coming to the store. *If on a Winter's Night a Traveler.* She realized that completing that transaction now would eat into her hour of computer time, so she decided to pick up the book afterwards.

To describe the connection on the old computer as 'spotty' was generous, in Tressa's opinion. After a series of starts and stops, and considerable waiting, she was finally able to open her email, and sure enough, a message dated three days earlier was waiting in her inbox from Rico. It was short and cautious, as hers had been, but Tressa convinced herself, after reading it six times, that he too was opening the door wide for them to resume this thing – whatever that was – between them.

Tressa!

So good to hear from you. I have been thinking about you constantly over the past few months, wondering how you are coping. I cannot begin nor would I be so arrogant as to pretend to imagine your sorrow over this ordeal.

Yes, a strong coffee sipped slowly over an overdue conversation would be wonderful. Just tell me when and where and I will be there. So glad to be in touch again.

He signed it simply, "Rico," without any closing, but she was convinced the message's sentiment held out more promise. Tressa began to compose a response, this time with fewer filters and less caution, but still within the realm of decency and good taste. Midway through her message, the connection was lost and the computer became frozen. Tressa went to get the bookseller girl, to see if she could help her reboot the machine, but the counter was unmanned, and she saw no one there but customers. Tressa wondered what had happened to the longhaired storeowner in the leather vest. She went back to her station to retrieve her coffee and noticed a cubicle behind the magazine racks that had been hidden from view.

Hoping against reasonable hope that she might find another computer, Tressa slipped behind the makeshift partition – really a wall made from boxes of magazines – and sat down in the rather posh leather office chair that was parked at that station. She had to laugh when she realized that she was actually sitting in front of a microfilm machine, something she had not seen in ages. Motivated purely by a sense of nostalgia, Tressa sat down at the machine, found the 'on' switch, and the machine whirred to life, illuminating the blank, yellowish screen. Tressa looked around the desk for a film to put on the spindle and eventually found a cardboard box filled with smaller boxes containing films to the left of her feet. She opened one of the microfilm boxes that bore a simple, typed label: "Scientific Voyager." After pulling out the glass tray from underneath the lens, Tressa placed the spool of microfilm on the spindle and deftly threaded it under the rollers and onto the take-up reel on the other side. She then wound the take up reel gently and pressed the red fast-forward button a few times to call up an image.

As easy as it was for her to set up the machine, it was far more difficult to manipulate it, despite her romanticized view over the past few years that these older vehicles of technology had something special to offer. Tressa had to laugh at her sense of nostalgia as she struggled to control the speed with which the machine carried her through the images, as well as to orient or zoom in on any particular image. Not to mention the fact that she had to rotate the document first, and ignore the imprinted image of a film reel that ran vertically along the border. Certainly *dogpile.com* or *Ask Jeeves* was more efficient than this. As the name on the reel suggested, she had chosen a science periodical. Not being much of a science buff, she was about to give up and look for another film when something caught her eye. It was an article entitled, "Reach out and touch someone...even if they are beyond your reach." The article began by talking about twin studies, something that had always intrigued Tressa since she and Liza were twins. (Although Liza liked to remind her that she was born a full two and a half minutes earlier.) The basic scientific precept, as far as Tressa could understand, was the idea that once particles have interacted, they will remain entwined or connected in some way. Any space that comes between two objects does not necessarily separate those objects. The article tied in this sub-discipline of quantum physics, known as "quantum entanglement" to the twin study, but did not stop there. Most of the anecdotal data was not new: stories of twins separated in early childhood or at birth, who, upon reuniting as adults, had lived eerily parallel lives. What was new and intriguing to Tressa was the undertaking of a select group of scientists to prove these sorts of connections in a methodical and logical way. Under the umbrella of this idea, these same theorists were exploring the idea that two people, who shared a connection, either biologically or through a strong bond of love, could feel a range of emotions, thoughts, and even physical sensations that affected the other, even if they were not within close, physical proximity to each other. Even if, to use the scientific term cited in the article, "locality" was not present. Under the last paragraph was a grainy picture of Albert Einstein and Niels Bohr with a caption about Einstein's dismissal of quantum entanglement, as "spooky action at a distance." The article digressed slightly, by way of providing a context for quantum theory.

Tressa did not have a frame of reference for the physics aspect of the article. Much of what was discussed in terms of quantum physics or quantum mechanics vacillated somewhere between undecipherable abstractions or as pure fantasy. Still, one idea presented in this article, an interpretation of quantum theory in the 1950s by a scientist named Hugh Everett, held her attention. Known as the "Many Worlds Theory," it proposed that there is a corresponding physical reality to every possibility in a quantum wave function. Thus, with every so-called "quantum event," such as particles interacting, the universe will actually split into alternative realities. Each of these realities presents a different outcome that is not only possible; in this alternate reality, it actually exists. Tressa mused about the implications of such an idea, wondering, if this were true on more than a theoretical level, whether these parallel existences just explode into being sporadically, or if there could be outside, human influences that could determine them. She couldn't quite put her finger on what it was about this theory that intrigued her so much but decided to print out the article to read later at her leisure. As the machine dinged and sputtered out the pages, Tressa re-read the first part of the article on twins and quantum entanglement.

Over the years, Tressa had moved away from her church for a variety of reasons, and had reached the conclusion that the only rock solid entities in which she had real faith these days were her love for her children, and her connection to her sister Liza. Long ago, Tressa had given up trying to explain the seemingly supernatural bond to her twin in a rational manner. As children, Tressa and Liza often would spontaneously finish each other's sentences, or verbally complete what had only been a thought in the other's mind. Then there was the time that Tressa collapsed, inexplicably, in a Cross Country race, feeling a shooting pain in her left knee. The school nurse examined her and found nothing. Later that evening, when Tressa finally made it home, she learned that a speeding taxi had run a red light and grazed Liza's bike in the process, knocking her to the ground. Liza had been taken to the emergency room where she was x-rayed and found to have a broken knee, the left one.

As adults, over the past years, the two sisters would often call each other, in anticipation of the other's need to talk. They had even bought matching outfits completely by chance, while separated geographically by more than a thousand miles, showing up for family reunions wearing the exact blouse and skirt, or dress, and shoes, without having consulted each other. Sometimes the colors would be different: Tressa would have the black shirt and white skirt and Liza would have the opposite, but the style, pattern, and designer would be identical. Overall, it was just a feeling that the sisters were always connected. A feeling that would only be duplicated for Tressa when she became a mother and often could sense injuries, illnesses, or emotional pain in her children, even before outward signs became evident.

Tressa closed her eyes for a moment and wondered if Ellis could feel her right now. Despite whatever had happened to him, she found herself hoping and praying that he could feel her love for him and know that nothing in this world was worth more to her than having him back in her life again. And, of course, having him be well. The fear that had been slowly creeping up on her in the past few months was that she felt her connection to Ellis shorting out. Hours would go by without her thinking about him. It would hit her, suddenly, and she would feel an immediate sense of shame and betrayal, as though she had let a light burn out that was supposed to guide her son back home.

Sighing and feeling a tremendous sense of heaviness, Tressa removed the microfiche reel with the science article and placed it in its container before returning it to the rather dog-eared cardboard box. She was about to return the entire box to its original hiding place when she spotted a curious label on another nearby box: "Real–life recordable reels." She pulled this box up onto the desk and then absentmindedly lifted her head and looked around as if she suddenly realized she might be doing something she was not supposed to. A quick scan of the bookstore revealed that it was still moving at the same languid pace she had observed earlier. No customers or store employees seemed interested in anything located in her semi-secluded corner. Tressa pulled out one of the 'recordable' films from the new box, and repeated her previous motions of threading it and calling up an image. This time, instead of an image, a single caption filled the screen.

TO PROCEED, PRESS THE RED BUTTON.

Tressa reluctantly pressed the red button, worried that she might cause damage to the machine since she was quite sure that fast-forward should not be engaged once an image was visible. The screen then flashed a new image and Tressa started to question her memory of how these microfilm machines worked. Was it possible to reach a new image without manually scrolling? Before she had time to reason this out, she found herself a victim of her curiosity, blindly following orders the machine was churning out:

PRESS FOREHEAD ON BAR ABOVE SCREEN AND ROTATE DIAL ONE COMPLETE TURN.

Tressa chuckled to herself, took a sip of her latte and pressed her head forward, as she would for a vision test. Obediently, she reached over and rotated the dial until she had made a complete circle. No sooner had she taken her hand off the dial that a flash of light from the screen alerted her to a new screen image:

THIS IS YOUR LIFE. REVIEW AND PRESS THE GREEN BUTTON TO CONTINUE.

Tressa felt a clamminess wash over her as the machine was suddenly loaded with a series of familiar photographic images. Like an automaton, she scrolled quickly at first, and then more slowly as she tried to process what she was looking at.

They were photos from her own life. Childhood photos with her sister Liza, wearing matching overalls at their grandparents' farm, with her parents and Liza around the family Christmas tree, and on the beach. Tressa stopped scrolling and again looked around her as though someone was waiting around the corner, ready to jump out and explain this elaborate prank. There was nobody within range. She then picked up the box that had had housed the film. Besides the hand-typed label, the box did not provide her with any more information. Tressa eyed her latte suspiciously, wondering if someone had slipped some sort of hallucinogen into her cup, and then dismissed the idea as ludicrous. Although, she reasoned, it was no more ludicrous than what she had encountered on that machine.

Tressa returned to her scrolling and found more photos of herself: as a teen with her Cross Country teammates, with her prom date pinning on a corsage. Many of these images were familiar, but she could not be sure that she had ever even seen hem before. As she scrolled on, photos popped up with Daniel at various stages during their courtship and then on their wedding day. The next frames after the eries of wedding shots were photos of their children. She looked first for all the pictures of Kassie: the smiling, chubby toddler who hardly resembled the roller-skate skinny version of her daughter as a young girl and teen. Tressa laughed as she hought of that term, "roller-skate skinny," taken from J.D. Salinger's *Catcher in the Rye*. Ellis had used that term to describe his sister after reading the iconic novel in his Freshman English class.

Swallowing hard, Tressa turned her focus to the photos of Ellis. The tender, sweet smile that would hardly change throughout his life was already evident in his earliest baby pictures. As she scrolled from one screen to another, she revisited many of the same photos she had been poring over devotedly for the past year. She was so hypnotized by this cottony fugue of memories and images that the very feasibility of all of this, or what it all meant, receded to the back of her consciousness. That is, until a new series of images popped up that Tressa did not recognize. Initially, she thought they must belong to someone else and was about to scroll to another screen when she saw that telltale arch in one eyebrow. It took her a moment, but then she asked herself aloud,

Is that...Ellis?

It was Ellis, but with a sallow expression, slightly sunken cheeks, his hair somewhat longer – though neatly trimmed, but overall looking somewhat unkempt now as facial hair colonized his once pristine milk and honey skin. Behind him a sign read,

Extra shot of espresso – .50

Shot of soy – .40

Ellis was flanked on either side by two young people that looked familiar. Tressa was sure she had encountered these kids, perhaps even spoken with them while on her mission to find Ellis out West. The two in the photo had been quick to say they knew her son, but at the same time, neither knew nor seemed to care what had become of him. Ellis's mouth was twisted into what anyone else would have mistaken as a smile, but it did not reflect even a hint of the joy and lightness that was integral to Ellis's nature.

Perplexed, Tressa moved to the next image, which this time was set on a busy street corner in a city she did not recognize, but that made her think of California from the abundant sunlight that permeated the frame. Ellis was standing on a corner, waiting for something or someone, his head only turned slightly as if someone had just called his name. He seemed unaware that his photo was being taken. His face, somewhat gaunt and certainly more careworn than in the previous shot, revealed an unidentifiable pain. A slight wrinkle in his forehead suggested a possible reaction to looking into the light, but Tressa interpreted it as more likely stemming from discomfort or anxiety.

Tressa let go of the dial and sank into her chair which wheeled backwards slightly in return. The clamminess she had felt earlier had now developed into a searing heat that quickly spread from her palms to her arms, her stomach, back and legs until she felt as though she was bathed in sweat. She stood up and pulled off her trench coat and the wool sweater she had been wearing underneath, which now smelled ever so slightly like wet dog. Still burning up, Tressa grabbed her bag, sweater and coat, but left her coffee, and went to the counter to buy a bottle of water. The owner of the store, still wearing his black leather vest and possibly the same striped shirt of a few days ago, was now manning the counter. He was filling a bowl with cat food on the floor while a grey tabby looked on expectantly. The bowl read, "Schrödinger," which Tressa thought an odd and rather cumbersome name for a pet. The man with the ponytail was stroking the cat's head and making affectionate kissing sounds. He looked up in surprise when Tressa gently cleared her throat. Before Tressa had a chance to order her water, the man showed an instant flicker of recognition and reached under the counter to produce a book that had a brown paper bag folded around it and secured with a rubber band. The bag had the name NOVAK written on the outside.

"Calvino's *If on a Winter's Night a Traveler...* Right?"

He rattled off the title with a slight air of theatrical exaggeration. It was not hard to understand why her aunt Regina felt right at home in this place.

"Yes," Tressa stammered, her voice cracking as though it had been weeks since she had spoken a word to another human being.

"It's been paid for, so you're all set." The man removed the rubber band and the bag and placed them in a tray next to the register before he handed the book to Tressa. He turned his back and was about to leave the counter when Tressa finally managed to utter her request for a bottle of water.

"I don't sell water by the bottle here, but I'll do you one better. Boston's finest: on the house."

He served her a glass of ice water from the tap with a warm, though not expansive, smile that revealed slightly tobacco-stained teeth.

"Oh, well, thank you. Yes, that's fine." Tressa took a drink, and then put her finger up in the air as though she had just remembered something:

"That microfilm machine in the back of the room, I..."

"Oh, don't worry, Miss. I don't charge for that – there's no demand. Only for the computers."

"Yes, but I wanted to tell you something..."

Tressa suddenly was overcome with feelings of tremendous self-doubt about what she had just seen projected on the old machine. Maybe she was under the influence of a high fever. Even without the trench coat and wool sweater, Tressa's body was still radiating an incendiary heat. Could she have completely imagined that spontaneous slideshow? It was too absurd to be real. Tressa wanted to ask, but she could not form the words. Instead, she dabbed the perspiration above her lip with a napkin she had taken from the counter and simply told the man that she had forgotten to put away the microfilm. In that moment, Tressa was too afraid to walk back to that dark corner and look at the screen of that machine. She was not sure what scared her more: the possibility of seeing those enigmatic snapshots that only moments ago had filled her with an indescribable anguish, or, seeing nothing but a blank screen. The man reassured her that he would take care of putting away the film, and reiterated that it was not a big deal; it was unlikely anyone would want to use the microfilm machine today, or any day in the near future.

"In fact,"

He added,

"If it weren't such a damn hassle to move that clunky thing, I'd probably have gotten rid of it by now. Don't suppose you'd like to make me an offer to take that contraption off my hands?"

Tressa just smiled weakly and placed the book on top of her purse before putting her trench coat on. She still felt overheated and could not face wearing the sweater that she now draped carelessly over her arm.

The man continued.

"No? Well enjoy your book. Good day for reading. Rainy days are always better than snowy ones. You from around here? No? Well, you are here for a historic dry spell for this time of year. Not for the rain, which is unseasonal, but no snow. Usually by now, we would see some snow. Some say it's some kind of millennial augury."

"I don't believe in all that nonsense."

Tressa said, buttoning her trench coat, and added,

"Thanks for the water."

The man nodded and flicked his hand upwards in a slightly dramatic gesture that seemed to mime both *goodbye* and *my pleasure*, before turning his attention back to Schrödinger the cat.

Once outside, Tressa inhaled deeply, and drank in the coolness and dampness of the weather she had found so brutal less than an hour earlier. The rain had slowed down to a freezing drizzle, and she briefly lifted her head and closed her eyes, enjoying the cool, gentle, pelting of the droplets on her cheeks, nose, and forehead. Tressa decided that she could not face the stuffiness or nauseating motion of a bus, or the jarring stop and go of a taxi. Instead, confident enough that she could make her way back to her aunt's apartment on foot, she pulled out her small, laminated map of Boston and started off.

3

Tressa did not know how long she had slept, since she had fallen asleep in darkness, and she now awoke to a completely dark apartment as well. When she had returned from her successful, though somewhat long and laborious trek back from the bookstore, the curtains and shades were still drawn in Regina's apartment. She had first peeked in on Regina, who was still sleeping, and, upon confirmation, also still breathing. This time, Regina's cats meowed faintly at Tressa, and she propped open the door to let them out into the apartment. Tressa quickly refilled the cats' water and food bowls, finding the aroma of the dried cat food almost too powerful to bear in her nauseated condition. Tressa had then left her bag on the kitchen table, along with her trench coat, which she peeled off as though it were a decaying skin, and proceeded to pull of all of her other clothes en route to the guest bedroom. Now, completely naked, she crawled into her bed, covering her searing skin with the cool relief of the sheet, and kicking the heavy quilt and fleece blanket to join her discarded garments on the floor.

When she awoke, Tressa felt somewhat cooler, although not as chilled as she might have expected. Tressa dragged herself out of bed, motivated not by a desire to do so, but by a lingering anxiety that had gotten the better of her and had finally woken her up.

Tressa did not feel up to facing the bright overhead light, and the lamp on her end table emitted a strange smell of old syrup when she turned it on, so she slowly sifted through her suitcase in the dark. She managed to find a pair of underwear, jeans, a long-sleeved t-shirt and some cotton socks. She pulled her watch off the end table but could not read the dial, so she shoved it in the front pocket of her jeans and trudged to the bathroom in the hall, still naked and shaky, holding her clothes pressed close to her. The bathroom light fixture protested loudly to Tressa turning it on, and like every other light in this otherwise dark cavern, shone with an unbearable fluorescence. Tressa took a quick look at her watch: 3:30. Was it a.m. or p.m.? She had no idea. She then turned the light back off and took a shower in the dark.

The pipes continued to rattle for at least five minutes after Tressa had turned off the water in the bathroom and Tressa was sure that her aunt would wake up from this sound. She dressed quickly, noticing that her clothes felt cool on her skin. She was not sure if her shower had been too hot, or if she was still feverish. Tressa crept back into her aunt's room, feeling like a negligent caregiver for having gone to sleep rather than helping her ill and aged aunt. To her surprise, Regina's bed was now empty, except for the cats who had assumed their mistress's spot. The shades and curtains were still drawn, however, which Tressa found disconcerting. Tressa's mother had always been vigilant about warding off mold, and it had been a fundamental rule in their household to open all curtains first thing in the morning, and not pull them shut again until the last light of day had faded. Opening them provided Tressa with resolution about the time on her watch: 4:00 p.m. Outside it was still grey, and growing dark, but not night yet. She had only slept for a couple of hours. Tressa saw the aspirin on her aunt's bedside table, grabbed the bottle and shook out a couple. She headed to the kitchen to wash them down with a glass of water and was stopped by a note that Regina had fixed with a simple magnet to the metal cabinet above the sink.

My Dear Tressa,

I ran out to get some more remedies for this nasty bug. Sorry to see it has knocked you down as well. Make sure you take something for that fever, and drink some orange juice. I will return shortly.

Auntie R.

Tressa obediently poured herself some orange juice and washed the aspirin down with considerable effort. Her throat felt raw, as though lined with barbs and thorns. So, she *was* ill, quite possibly very ill. If that was the explanation for her experience in the bookstore, she might be in trouble. How high was her fever, anyway? She decided she needed to find a thermometer as soon as possible. Rooting through the medicine and kitchen cabinets yielded no results. Tressa was not surprised; Regina had such a casual, no-fuss attitude when it came to her health, the presence of a thermometer in that household would have been completely out of place. It was a miracle Regina even had aspirin, considering all of the high-proof liquid remedies that lined her shelves and most likely served her for most ailments and illnesses.

Tressa did not know what to do with herself; she felt so out of sorts. For once, she was not fixated on the ongoing tragedy of her real life; instead, she was distressed by her experience earlier that day. Tressa decided to retreat to her bed with the new book. She walked over the table to retrieve it from her bag, but to her horror, it was not there. She had been so certain that she had put it there. But then, she thought to herself dubiously, she had also been certain of seeing and doing other things in that bookstore that made no rational sense whatsoever. She emptied the entire contents of the bag and discovered with a slight sense of shame that the reservation pod was still in her purse. She returned the pod, her wallet, a few items of makeup and her hairbrush back to her bag and then moved on to look in the pockets of her trench coat, even though it defied all logic that the book could have fit there without sustaining serious damage, something of which she had always been mindful. This, like the opening of drapes every morning, was another legacy of her mother's: treating books as though they were old friends. She was always careful to make sure that the cover, spine, and individual pages of any book did not get damaged or compromised in any way.

As Tressa rearranged her coat on the back of Regina's dining room chair, she realized that her wool sweater was also missing. She followed the trail of socks, chino slacks, matching silk panties and camisole, and the rayon peasant shirt to her bed, and even shook out the blankets from the floor, but the sweater was nowhere to be found. This caused her a certain amount of pain since she had not packed another warm sweater, and since that particular one had such sentimental value. She had had that sweater since she was a teen, a gift from her grandmother who had knit it herself. It dawned on her that she must have dropped both her sweater and the book at the Underground Traveler. She would not allow herself to contemplate the possibility that she had dropped and lost them both on her feverish trek from the bookstore back to her aunt's home.

With great effort, Tressa pulled on her still slightly damp coat, and slipped into some dry clogs, the only other shoes she had brought. As almost an afterthought, Tressa grabbed one of Regina's many silk scarves from the coat rack next to the front door, and arranged it around her neck and chest to ward off the cold and damp.

Once outside, Tressa decided again to forego the various forms of rapid transit since the dizziness, nausea and general malaise of earlier were still lingering. She was determined that she could walk this thing off, and convinced she could retrace her steps from earlier. The rain had stopped altogether, and once again, Tressa found the sharp chill of the air incredibly refreshing, even soothing. She found herself craving even a momentary cloudburst to moisten and cool her burning skin.

Note to self, I must rehydrate.

She found herself saying,

Ok, now I know that I am delusional. I am walking down a street in Boston, talking to myself, while on my way to a creepy bookstore that smells like oil or paraffin, or some other odd, anachronistic scent, to retrieve items I lost while fleeing from a machine that sent me messages and photos of my lost son. Is this a breakdown? Is this what that feels like?

Tressa's monologue trailed off as she just barely managed to dodge a careening motorist who was flying at highway speed down the neighborhood side street she had been following. As though frozen in time, Tressa stood in the street afterwards, watching the driver lower his raised fist that had been shaking unspoken obscenities at this obvious out-of-towner.

Tressa then passed a woman on the street struggling with her two young children. The young woman, who looked older than her years, was obviously in a hurry, and was becoming increasingly impatient with the two not-quite-school aged tots who were trotting to keep up with their mother who occasionally turned her head around and barked a reminder to *keep up!* as she quickened her pace.

Tressa always regarded such scenes with a tremendous amount of ntrospection. Many of her friends, including her own sister, were quick to pass mmediate and unwavering judgment on displays of questionable parenting, but Tressa always started to script a backstory in her head, trying to imagine and sort out what pushes all of us at times to act differently than we would like to or should. In the fiction she was crafting around this unknown woman, Tressa imagined that she had been abandoned recently by her husband, and now had to work three jobs to support her children. As she continued to envisage this fictional scenario, Tressa imagined that the woman usually brought the kids to a babysitter, but today, the babysitter was sick, and the woman was virtually alone in Boston because all her family still lived in her Midwestern hometown. The woman had moved to Boston with her husband shortly after they married. So now, the young mother was forced to drag the kids along to her second shift job at the dry cleaners, where she was worried both about their safety and the jeopardy it might bring to her own employment status there...

This caused Tressa to reflect, as so many of these fictional musings often did, on her own life, and she was reminded of a dark time over eleven years ago – which, until Ellis's disappearance, she had always regarded as the darkest period of her life – when she was convinced that she and Daniel would certainly break up for good. Tressa had gone as far as hiring a divorce attorney, and taking the kids to stay with Liza temporarily, after Daniel had admitted to an affair with a younger colleague at work.

At some point, Daniel had a pang of conscience and broke off what had been an eighteen-month relationship with this other woman abruptly. This had left the young and beautiful other woman, whose name was Claire, seething, bitter, and hell bent on some sort of extramarital vengeance. Claire sent Tressa a long letter, outlining every detail of her affair with Daniel.

Somehow, through brief counseling, and displays of contrition and penitence on Daniel's part, as well as a whole lot of mind control on her part, Tressa managed to put that episode behind them, and move on, for the most part. Watching this harried woman with her children in tow reminded Tressa why she had decided to swallow her pride and save her marriage. Her decision was not motivated by the fear that she, like the quasi-fictional persona she had just envisioned, would end up poor and struggling, nor did she fear losing custody since she had incontrovertible truth of Daniel's transgressions. Instead, it was the thought that some other woman could have even a small role in her children's lives. That was somehow completely unacceptable to her. She had enough trouble relinquishing supervision of her children to trusted sitters, but she truly could not envision ceding their care for longer stretches to some stranger. She would swallow a thousand indignities and blows to her self-esteem before she would let that happen.

Tressa trudged on, far away from the woman and her children, loosening her aunt's scarf from the death grip she had initially arranged, still milling over all of these past conflicts and the pain that she had managed to keep at bay until Ellis's disappearance reopened every wound in her marriage. As she reflected on her life with Daniel, Tressa was reminded of the same fear she had first experienced as a teenager. When Tressa was only eighteen, she experienced a flash of existential angst that was the closest she would get to self-reflection before the age of twenty-five. It was her freshman year and she had fallen madly in love, or so she thought, to a fellow student from Georgia named Bill Fuller. Tressa had promised Bill the world, including an eventual marriage engagement. However, after Tressa and Bill had been together for about five months, she suddenly informed Bill that she did not love him, but that she did, in fact, love another boy she had just met at a party the previous weekend. The thing that struck her even then at that tender age, that scared her more than anything up to that point, was that she recognized in both of those relationships that she had *felt* the same: the same intensity of passion, the same sensation of boundless, undying love, and then, in the blink of an eye, she felt virtually nothing. Tressa started to wonder if she could turn her emotions on and off like a light switch. Or worse, if she could convince herself to feel whatever was convenient to feel in that particular moment. She could not reconcile this at the time, since she did feel so deeply when she was in the throes of whatever passionate relationship was in progress. This fleeting thought returned when she forgave Daniel for his affair and shabby disregard for her, and blindly and rather effortlessly moved on, as though none of it had ever even happened. She *had* to stay with him; they *had* to remain a family. She *had* to love him. Now, this thought returned with great force, seemingly out of nowhere, as she approached the intersection of Milk and India and spied the Underground Traveler's Bookstore up ahead. Had her rosy, dreamlike marriage to Daniel since that dark time really been more of a case of Stockholm Syndrome? Had she persuaded herself that she was deliriously happy and that their marriage was ideal, in order to survive? Did she ever really love Daniel, or feel she had to since she was carrying his child? And how did her simmering feelings for Rico Suarez fit into this model? Tressa was left with an unsettling numb feeling, not having any definitive answers to her own questions.

Tressa pulled open the door to the bookstore, and did not notice the chill inside as she had earlier in the day. She was, however, instantly hit by that same lingering odor of oil or resin. She was not sure what it was, but it reminded her of the characteristic odors that haunted her grandparents' one hundred year-old farm in Michigan. They were smells of natural resources, toil and sweat that belonged to a bygone era. Sensory markers that had been removed by several generations and replaced everywhere with indicators of industrial progress such as plastic, vinyl, and other synthetics. By contrast, the dense, hardwood floor of the *Underground*, which seemed to have shed all the wet footprints from the morning, looked as though it had weathered a century or two. Tressa approached the counter and greeted the same girl that had assigned her the computer with the 'spotty' internet service earlier that day. Tressa explained that she had lost both a book and a sweater, and the girl stared at her blankly for a moment before she dipped her head perfunctorily below the level of the counter and then rose with a blank expression and answered without ffect that no one had turned those things in. Tressa thanked her with a reciprocal lack of affect and decided to wander over to her computer station just in case she had left something there.

The Mac she had used sat idle, unplugged, apparently awaiting further technical attention. With great trepidation, Tressa walked over to the semi-hidden corner with the microfilm machine. Before she knew it, Tressa caught her clog on the tip of a nail head that was protruding ever so slightly from the floorboard. She began hurtling forward and just managed to catch herself before she fell face first into another stack of boxes. Otherwise unscathed by the fall, Tressa angrily picked up her shoe, holding her breath as she examined it for a tear. She found only an insignificant snag at the toe that she hoped would not get any worse.

She slipped back into her clog and made her way around this new wall of cardboard boxes, peering tentatively around the corner as though a growling beast were awaiting her. The screen of the outmoded machine was dark, so Tressa concluded that the man in the leather vest must have turned off the device. To her surprise, draped over the back of the rolling chair was her wool sweater, and sitting on the desk was her copy of the Calvino book.

The owner must have put them back.

Tressa had resumed her monologue from earlier, talking to no one, or perhaps to herself. She leaned forward and pulled the sweater from the chair, which sent it rolling into the desk. The slight nudge from the chair seemed to reawaken the sleeping machine.

This time Tressa noticed a low, constant, just barely audible hum that the "contraption," as the man had called it, was emitting. As the screen lit up, Tressa noticed there were no photos as there had been before – or as she had thought there had been – only a message similar to the previous two:

PRESS THE GREEN BUTTON FOR MORE TIME.

Tressa stood rooted to the spot for a series of protracted seconds. She finally gave in, leaned over, and pressed the green button, while still standing, the leather chair serving as some kind of buffer between her and the machine. The humming became just slightly louder, and suddenly the screen exploded with photos again. The images that popped up were in seemingly the same order as before: Tressa as a child – *scroll* – as a teen – *scroll* – with Daniel – *scroll* – her children as babies – *scroll* – Ellis on a sunny urban street corner. The sight of her son's lost, tender gaze filled her with pain. Tressa gingerly pulled out the chair, undid her coat, and placed it, her sweater, and the book – that she now placed back firmly in her purse – on the floor next to the chair before she sat down. She noticed something glowing in her bag, and realized that she had forgotten to turn in that stupid reservation pod again. She tucked it in the back pocket of her jeans and made a mental note to return it on her way out.

She then played with the auto-focus, hoping to zero in on some minor detail in that photo that was not obvious before. Instead, all the photos suddenly and spontaneously moved upwards, and a series of numbers and accompanying text filled the screen. The images had stopped moving, so Tressa again attempted to control the machine with the dial on the side. Scrolling up and down she soon realized that she was looking at a sort of timeline. The first year in the timeline was 1960, beginning with January 11, the date of her birth. Every subsequent year was listed with a complete twelve-month calendar. Within each month were dates, broken down by hours, formatted in the European twenty-four hour clock. Tressa stopped scrolling for a moment and sank backwards in the chair, still not sure of what she was dealing with. She bent over and pulled the café napkin out of her purse, and mopped some of the sweat from her forehead. Still feeling almost unbearably overheated, Tressa gently kicked off her clogs and pulled off her socks, reveling in the coolness of the floor. When she looked at the screen again, Tressa noticed for the first time that each year was framed in a box, and that a message had appeared at the top of the screen:

PRESS THE GREEN AND RED BUTTONS SIMULTANEOUSLY TO SELECT A MOMENT IN TIME. APPLY FOREHEAD TO BAR TO LOCK IN TIME.

PLEASE NOTE: ALL SEQUENCES HAVE A MAXIMUM SHELF LIFE OF THREE CALENDAR DAYS BEFORE CLOCK IS RESET

TO REAL TIME.

Tressa remained somewhat slouched in her chair, feeling a weariness creep over her that was spreading to every part of her body making her limbs feel unbearably heavy. She wondered if she would even have the strength to get up and find her way back again to her aunt's apartment.

Is this madness? Can delusions be this convincing?

Tressa sat upright with some effort and scrolled through the years with no particular interest, convinced that she had to be hallucinating, until one of the years caught her eye: 1980. The year she met Daniel. She scrolled gently and slowly, occasionally going back as the machine moved too quickly despite her efforts to control it. She was trying to land on January, the month when they had met. Tressa remembered the exact date, the eleventh, because it had also been her birthday. Like so many events that turn out to be life changing, their meeting had been completely by chance. It was Tressa's twentieth birthday, and she had planned to meet some friends from school at an old, local tavern that was actually below street level, and that served college kids without checking I.D.s, or at least that had been their unofficial policy. What Tressa and her three friends were unaware of was that local law enforcement had recently started to crack down on establishments serving alcohol to underage kids. This campaign was initiated after an eighteen-year old girl, an out-of-state freshman from Iowa, died from alcohol poisoning after allegedly doing an untold number of tequila shots followed by copious amounts of beer. Her parents had threatened to sue the university, county, the city, and the state, so the authorities had responded in an effort to mitigate the publicity and the fallout. While the campaign was not exactly a secret, it was not common knowledge either, and so those four unwitting girls started their descent to the bar on the cracked cement staircase that led from the street above. Midway down, Tressa remembered, she felt the hair stand up on the back of her neck. She could not put her finger on what was amiss, but she felt strongly that something was wrong. They had not quite reached the bottom step when a handsome young man with striking green eyes placed himself in their path.

"Hey, ladies. What took you so long?"

None of the girls knew him, as they confirmed from a few quick glances and shrugs, but there was something about his confident manner, and his clean-cut, athletic appearance that inspired complete trust. Or, perhaps it was the simple fact that they were four unattached girls facing a very attractive and seemingly available guy. He locked arms with Tressa and Alanna, one of her friends, and led all four of them – the two other friends following stupefied – away from the bar and down the subterranean alley to a Mexican restaurant on the other side. Once inside, the young man grabbed a few menus and nodded to the owner as he led them to a table. The five squeezed into a booth. Tressa spoke to him first, pointing to the restaurant owner as she asked,

'So, is this how you round up business for your boss?"

The young man laughed, his green eyes sparkling, and Tressa would always remember how in that moment, she did not know if she was irritated by this guy, or excited.

"No. I don't work here. I just come here a lot. Actually, I just saved your hides."

The girls giggled foolishly, but none of them except Tressa dared to speak. It was as though she had appointed herself as the leader and spokesperson for the group.

"Is that so? You mean, you saved us from having a great time? You saved me from celebrating my birthday with White Russians and Fuzzy Navels? Gee, thanks."

"No, I mean I saved you from the two undercover cops who were checking IDs of customers *after* they had already gotten their drinks. I had just watched one of them haul off three unsuspecting kids and was on my way out when I spotted the four of you and knew what you were about to walk into. By the way, I'm Daniel. And you are...?"

Tressa had offered Daniel her hand, and would always remember the involuntary blush and smile that took over her face as she thanked this charming stranger for being so gallant. Yes, that was the word she had used, *gallant.* She cringed at the memory of her twenty-year old self. That same night she wound up in bed with Daniel and from that point on, the rest of her fate was essentially sealed.

Tressa stared at the date she had finally managed to pull up on the computer: January 11, 1980. She played with the knob a bit to tweak the time and managed to land on 20:00. That was what she remembered, anyway, that she and the girls met that night after she got off work – she had a job in the main library on campus. She let go of the knob, and the border around the selected time and date pulsed faintly and slowly. Tressa closed her eyes for a moment and leaned back in the chair. She had the strange sensation she used to get immediately after a cross-country race as the buildup of heat and pressure slowly started to dissipate, somewhat like a hissing radiator. She wondered what, if anything, would happen if she were to press the green and red buttons simultaneously, and applied her forehead the way she had earlier that day. Would the machine show her more photos? Or, maybe, this time, a video reel? That was silly, considering there were very few home movies of her, and as far as she knew, they certainly did not predate her children's elementary school years when she and Daniel had bought their first video camera. Tressa reached into her bag and pulled out the same ratty napkin she had used earlier and again wiped her brow. Although she was still covered in perspiration, she had started to shiver from a chill that covered her body. She pulled her sweater back on, slid her bare feet into her clogs, and then pushed the red and green buttons with her still somewhat sweaty fingers, while pressing her damp forehead to the bar above the screen. Within a fraction of a second, Tressa was hit with what had all the indications of a migraine: a blinding flash of light accompanied by intense pain in her temples and the top of her head. She involuntarily squeezed her eyes shut and held her breath waiting for it to pass.

After a few moments, the pain and light could no longer get through, but she was overcome by a bone-numbing chill. Tressa opened her eyes and at first saw only darkness. She suddenly remembered that the *Underground* owner had warned her and Regina of the store's early closing at 6:00 on New Year's Eve. She felt a feeling of panic as she realized she might be locked in the store. She tried to get her bearings, but then realized that something, or everything, was different. Sounds, smells, the temperature of the air. Her body felt colder and somewhat heavier. Tressa lifted her hand from what she had thought was the arm of the chair, but, upon closer inspection, turned out to be an iron railing. Once her eyes adjusted to the lack of light, she realized that she was outside and standing on a cement staircase. There was only a dim light coming from the street above her. She stepped down to the last step and emitted what could best be described as a guffaw as she spotted a neon sign indicating, "He's Not Here." The bar from her college days.

4

It couldn't be.

Again, Tressa directed her monologue to no one in particular as she approached the window of the bar. Strains of Cheap Trick's *I want you to want me* filtered through the brick exterior. She tried to peer inside but did not see her friends, nor Daniel, nor anyone who might be an undercover cop. Tressa tried to look in the corner of the window, and was met with an image that vaguely resembled her reflection. It was as though she was looking at a picture of herself twenty years earlier.

She extended her arm in front of her face, pointing her hand towards the streetlight, and almost recoiled in terror. The protruding veins that had developed from years of running and workouts at the gym were not visible. Instead, her skin had an unusual cast, possibly from the greenish streetlight, but Tressa recognized that paleness from her youth. She put her hands on her face and kneaded it gently with her fingertips; it felt much fuller than usual. Slowly running her fingers from her forehead, down her nose, across her cheekbones, over her chin, her skin was definitely more pliant, softer, and oilier. Tressa looked down at her body and noticed the same wool sweater with the long-sleeved white t-shirt peeking out at the cuffs, jeans and clogs that she had pulled out of her suitcase today (*was that today?*), but the button on her jeans had popped open and she suddenly became very aware of how tight they felt. She self-consciously pulled her sweater down over the fly, leaving the button open, and decided to walk down the alley to see if the Mexican restaurant was still there. Sure enough, it was. Thick and dusty blinds covered the windows, so Tressa had to enter the restaurant to confirm her creeping suspicion that she was reliving that moment in time.

Sure enough, at the same booth she remembered from that fateful night, there sat Daniel with Tressa's three friends, all of whom were fawning over him, touching him, laughing a bit too loudly, tossing their hair just a bit too much. Blondie's *Heart of Glass* played in the background, and the girls were sporting either long feathered hairdos, or, as in the case of her friend Alanna, a tight and long permed style. Tressa reflexively ran her hand through her own hair. She cringed when her fingers met resistance with a mass of salon created curls.

"Tressa!"

Her friends called her over, and Daniel graciously stood up and offered her his seat before sliding in next to her. Tressa caught Alanna staring at her intensely in that ıoment, and was disarmed by what she saw flash in her friend's eyes: jealousy, ›ossibly even a warning – *this one is mine, I saw him first.* In that moment, Tressa aughed aloud at that idea. The girls all looked at her quizzically.

"Sorry, I just really don't get all this..."

The girls looked at their friend expectantly, waiting for her to elaborate, and Tressa ealized that whatever this was, dream or reality, she was experiencing it. Everything uggested it was very real. She could smell the grease from the kitchen, as well as Daniel's cologne. She felt a bit nauseated, possibly from the combination of odors, or, more likely, from what felt like the most vivid hallucination she could ever have magined. She explained to her friends, feeling in that moment as though she were being called upon to recite a line in a performance:

"I mean, I'm just confused. What are you guys doing here? Weren't we supposed to meet at *He's Not*?"

It was her friend Missy who answered:

"Oh, Tressa! There are undercover cops there busting underage drinking – can you believe that? Daniel, here ...Oh, I'm sorry. Daniel, this is our friend Tressa..."

Daniel pivoted slightly to his left and extended his right arm across his stomach, offering Tressa, who was sitting so close to him that they were already touching, a short, but firm handshake.

Missy continued,

"So, Daniel was outside the bar and saw us heading in that direction and *saved* us from walking right into that trap! Isn't that fantastic?"

"Fabulous."

Tressa answered drily. She took a deep breath and shut her eyes. When she opened them it was still, apparently, 1980, and she was sitting, in the body of her twenty-year old self, next to her future husband and father of her children.

'Right. OK."

Tressa muttered to herself.

"What's the matter?"

This was Alanna, who seemingly asked more out of annoyance than out of any real concern for her friend's well-being.

"Well, did it even occur to you all that I was still on my way, and that without any warning, I would have walked into that same trap?"

The girls said nothing, and Daniel looked uncomfortable.

"Sorry, Tress. We assumed you would wait for us outside, I guess. I don't know what we were thinking, actually."

This time it was Tanya, who had been sitting on the opposite, innermost part of the booth looking sheepish.

Daniel stepped in again, assuming his chivalrous role, one with which Tressa had become familiar over a virtual lifetime together with him.

"Well, you're here now, and that's what counts. I understand it's your birthday? How about some margaritas to celebrate? They're on me."

Daniel smiled warmly, and she found it hard to form the grimace that she knew would be appropriate in this situation. She had forgotten how charming he could be, or had been, anyway, at one time. She managed, just the same, to look annoyed, and waved her hand slightly in a sign of gentle rejection.

Daniel persisted, another aspect of his nature that Tressa had forgotten. The last ten or more years between them had been characterized by compromise, passive aggressive silence, or consent with teeth gritted.

"No, really, Tressa don't worry about it. Here, I can guarantee you, nobody will card you. I know the owner personally."

Before Tressa could correct him, that she was not afraid of being carded, but simply was not in the mood for margaritas, Daniel had waved over the waiter and ordered a pitcher for the five of them. Tressa was about to say something, but Alanna reached across the table and grabbed Daniel's hands in her own.

"You're so good to us!"

Alanna said this with a wink and a conspiratorial smile that was so obvious it made Tressa roll her eyes in disgust.

Tressa turned to Daniel and thanked him for the offer with a reserved cordiality, and motioned that she needed to get out of the booth. He stood up and watched her as she smoothed her sweater over the top of her jeans.

"Thanks, you guys, but I guess I am just not in a very festive mood tonight. You all go ahead and enjoy."

Her friends looked at her in disbelief, but only Tanya spoke:

"Don't go! Come on! We're sorry if you think we ditched you. Let us make it up to you. At least have one margarita!"

Tressa smiled at her friend's sincerity. She regretted that somehow she and Tanya had dropped out of contact more than fifteen years ago. As for the other girls, Alanna and Missy, Tressa had pretty much lost touch with them after she left school and Ellis was born. Looking at the dynamic now, she realized she had not even missed them. Tressa reassured Tanya one more time that she was fine, promising to call later that night, which she realized was an insane kind of promise to make. After all, where would she go from here? Back to her dorm apartment? She did not even have a key. In fact, it occurred to her, she had nothing: no ID, no money, and no keys.

She walked out of the restaurant and into the night, heading in the direction of campus, hoping that somehow this whole alternate universe that she had been plunged into would not swallow her up. As she walked down the street, feeling the chill mostly on her feet that were bare inside her clogs, she felt a strange vibrating sensation on her butt. She reached back and palpated something hard in her back pocket. She pulled it out: it was the reservation pod from the *Underground* bookstore, humming softly.

How did I not feel this?

She wondered, but then looking down at her expansive thighs, (she had always been so much heavier before the birth of her two children) she realized that in this parallel universe she had more padding back there than she had been accustomed to for a couple of decades now. She was about to put the device back when she noticed that the red lights located in each of the four corners were flashing.

Great. Now my computer is ready.

She laughed again, but then noticed that there were words in the middle of the device.

POSSIBLE LIFE-ALTERING ACTIVITY INITIATED.PRESS THE CENTER OF THE SCREEN TO SEE THIS THROUGH.TIME REMAINING FOR THIS

SEQUENCE: 71 HOURS, 15 MINUTES. SHAKE THE DEVICE TO LOCATE NEAREST RETURN PORTAL.

Life altering activity.

Tressa pondered the implications of this. She had no clue how much of this was real and how much was feverish delirium. She also could not wrap her head around what this message was, but focusing on the words "RETURN PORTAL," she shook the device. Another message popped up:

NEAREST RETURN PORTAL: .5 miles PHOTO BOOTH. STUDENT UNION.

The device then went to black, the text vanished, and the red lights went out.

Rather certain that she still remembered where the landmark buildings were located at her alma mater, Tressa cut across the campus, something she used to do routinely after dark as an immortal twenty-year old. Her middle-aged soul, however, was on full alert as she quickened her pace, scanning the area, and she attempted to stay within the swath illuminated by the streetlamps. When she spotted the Student Union about 500 yards away, she broke into a sprint, a pace she had not been capable of maintaining in the past three years since arthritis had slowly been attacking her joints. Now, however, Tressa found she could run with a swiftness and ease she had long since forgotten, if it were not for her clunky shoes. She removed the clogs and carried them as she ran, effortlessly, as though she could run forever.

;he had tremendous wind, and even greater flexibility in her joints than she could emember having had for ages. She had to laugh at the twenty-year old version of ıerself who was slightly plump and had never taken full advantage of the suppleness ınd boundless energy in this youthful body.

Feeling victorious, Tressa ran up the stairs of the building, tempted to do a :eremonial Rocky Balboa dance, but instead, slipped into her clogs and walked nside. Two young people stared at her with somewhat puzzled expressions, and Tressa realized her face was radiating a kind of exuberance that usually was only present when foreign substances, alcohol, or sex were involved.

Let them think what they want to!

She laughed to herself, and asked at the front desk if there was a photo booth somewhere in the building. The kid behind the counter, who had been reading and highlighting Rousseau's *Confessions*, eyed Tressa curiously, as though he wanted to ask her, *Are you high?*

Instead, he directed her to the bowling alley on the lower level. There was a photo booth down there, near the shoe rental counter.

Tressa descended the overheated, stuffy stairwell and entered the bowling alley, a place she could not ever remember having frequented while a student here. She looked around. It was rather empty, just a few kids and some couples who seemed more interested in sneaking in gropes and passionate kisses between sets.

Tressa headed for the shoe rentals and found the photo booth immediately. She glanced underneath the curtain before she pulled it back to make sure no one was in there. Once inside, she closed the curtain, and looked around. The hard metal stool, the silver colored curtain on the back wall, and the oversized lettering spelling out, "PHOTOS," in different primary colors on the machine itself brought back a flurry of memories. Not from college, but from her high school days: Tressa with Liza, Tressa with friends, or Tressa with whatever boyfriend she was with at the time, cramming into the photo booth and trying to align their faces within the box that would frame the shot. Usually, either the top of the head or everything below the chin was missing in the final shot, someone miscalculating the adjustment of the stool. Tressa found herself suddenly feeling rather ridiculous, although, she reasoned, the whole experience was absurd. Which part of this was the least outrageous? There she was, standing in her twenty-year old body at her old campus bowling alley in a photo booth alone on a Friday night hoping to be beamed back to the right decade, and, within a day, the current millennium. At that moment, the device in her back pocket started to whir and vibrate again. Tressa reached back and pulled it out. The red lights had returned and were pulsing steadily. A message appeared again in the center of the screen:

> INSERT THREE QUARTERS IN THE MACHINE. SELECT BLACK AND WHITE IMAGE. REMAIN SEATED ON STOOL THROUGHOUT TRANSPORT.

Tressa instinctively began to root around in her jeans pockets, but she already knew that she had no dollars or coins. All her money was in her purse hundreds of miles, or more appropriately, hundreds of thousands of hours away.

For the first time since she had embarked on this journey, if that was, in fact, the appropriate term to use, Tressa began to feel a weariness combined with helplessness.

Maybe this is more than a feverish delirium; maybe I am in a coma…

She had read tales of coma victims who slip off into another world that feels, smells, and *is* as real to them as the actual world keeping vigil around their hospital bed. If that were the case, three quarters were surely not going to be enough to pull her out of this state.

She decided she had to try. She looked in the mirror in the photo booth and wished that she at least had a comb. Her hair looked a bit disheveled. As for her face, she had very little makeup on, and could have maybe used some face powder, but, despite the baby fat, Tressa would have happily taken her younger face with her into the next millennium if she could have. Feeling as though she had just shed two decades from her old, tired self, she boldly walked over to the only group of all males who were bowling on the last lane. The two boys were drinking cokes, which, judging from the delicious odor that wafted up from their cans, were spiked with Jack Daniels. This had not been her original plan, but she brazenly asked one of the boys for a sip. She said it after licking her lips demonstratively. One young college student, gangly, bespectacled, and suffering from a severe acne problem, laughed nervously and said loudly,

"You want a taste of my coke? Yeah, sure!"

"Craig, you're an idiot!" Slurred his friend, who was considerably more attractive, although also thin and untoned. Bowling was probably the height of athleticism for these two.

Tressa unabashedly took a few gulps of the drink, which instantly made her feel better. Her muscles seemed to relax, the knot in her stomach disappeared, and the despair of moments earlier seemed to evaporate.

If this is a coma, I hope I can remember to tell someone about these vivid sensory perceptions.

"Tell you, what…" She began, suddenly struck by a new way to hit them up for seventy-five cents.

"If you give me the money, I'll buy myself a coke, and then we can go to my dorm room to party."

Tressa thought the youth with the glasses would choke on the gulp of Jack and Coke he had just taken, but he did not hesitate to answer with a hearty "Yes!" He handed her two quarters.

"What's this?" She asked.

"Fifty cents for the coke?" The boy said, suddenly looking concerned that his girl might not be all there.

Tressa had forgotten how much, or rather, how little, things had cost twenty years ago. Basking in this ephemeral state of being a young seductress, however, Tressa did not lose a moment before she recovered:

"Why don't you give me a dollar instead, and I'll bring a friend along too?"

Tressa assured them she would be right back and headed to the photo booth with the four quarters the eager young men had provided.

Repeating the same steps as before – peeking under the curtain, closing the curtain, sitting down on the stool, leaning forward – Tressa put three of the four quarters in the machine and then remembered that she was supposed to select the black and white image from the choices. She stood up slightly, still bent forward, her butt still hovering over the stool, and entered her choice. The machine immediately started to beep loudly. It was a sound that Tressa recognized as being eerily anachronistic: the discordant but unmistakable sounds of a dial-up internet modem. Tressa quickly sat down a bit too hard so that she felt the presence of the restaurant reservation-cum-time travel device in her back pocket. Blinding light filled the booth and Tressa shut her eyes hard. She did not have the sensation of moving, but she felt her stomach sink to her ankles; similar to what she would occasionally feel riding in an elevator. Then, everything was quiet and she felt herself fall.

5

Tressa opened her eyes and noticed she was on the floor of the Underground Traveler, inches away from the microfilm machine. The lights were still on. Tressa walked on what felt like wobbly sea legs towards the middle of the store. Looking around, Tressa was able to confirm that the store had not yet closed. A handful of people were parked at computers, and three others were sitting at the counter sipping their coffee and reading magazines or books. Tressa hurried back to the machine, hoping for a clue, or some confirmation that she had not imagined the whole thing. At first, there was nothing, and the machine, in fact, seemed to be turned off. She remembered the last time when the machine woke up from the jarring motion of the rolling office chair. She pushed the chair back into the desk expecting the same result, but the machine remained idle with a blank, dark screen. Tressa raised her hand to her head. She felt somewhat clammy, but no longer sweaty or feverish. Determined to find some resolution – although she was uncertain what ind she was looking for – Tressa pulled the reservation pod out of her pocket. It too was blank. She tapped it with no result. Then she shook it. Still nothing. She flung it on the desk in irritation and sank into the office chair. No sooner did the pod make contact with the desk that the microfilm machine came back to life, flashing a message in the center of the screen. Tressa felt a wave of inexplicable and irrational relief as she was once again dialed into the *system*? *Network*? She had no appropriate vocabulary for what all of this was:

> PRESS GREEN BUTTON WITH LEFT HAND TO SEE POSSIBLE SIDEBARS OF LAST TRAVEL SEQUENCE. PRESS RED BUTTON FOR HELP. PRESS RED AND GREEN BUTTON TO LOCK IN CHOICE. PRESS GREEN BUTTON WITH RIGHT HAND TO SELECT NEXT TRAVEL SEQUENCE.

Sidebar? Tressa was puzzled by this term. She pressed the red button for help, and an explanation of *sidebar* in this context was revealed:

> SIDEBARS ARE THE POSITIVE AND/OR NEGATIVE CONSEQUENCES OF ONE'S ACTIONS FOLLOWING A TIME TRAVEL SEQUENCE. PLEASE NOTE: THESE ARE NOT COMPLETE DISCLOSURES. LIMITED INFORMATION IS AVAILABLE. TRAVELERS MUST DECIDE

WHETHER OR NOT TO LOCK IN ALTERNATE REALITIES BASED ON THEIR UNDERSTANDING OF THE INFORMATION GIVEN.

Tressa did not question the authenticity of any of this. For the first time, it all seemed to make sense in some odd, surreal way. She pressed the green button with her left middle finger, eager to see if she had actually gone anywhere, changed anything. As she did so, she noticed that her wedding ring was missing. She tried to remember if she had taken it off while showering at her aunt's house.

Come to think of it, I did not have it on my journey to 1980 when I looked at my hand in the glow of the streetlight next to the campus bar.

Within seconds, a flurry of pictures with captions filled the screen. What struck Tressa immediately was what was *not* there. No pictures this time of Daniel, nor of Ellis, and none of Kassie. There were many pictures, however, of Tressa: dressed smartly, wearing what were obviously very expensive, designer suits. Her skin was glowing, her hand that was brushing the hair out of her face in one windy shot, was adorned with perfectly manicured nails, and a few shimmering baubles that looked like real gems. She was with people she did not recognize, all of whom were also well dressed and coiffed. They all were smiling, but Tressa still did not perceive a feeling of true happiness or lightness in any of these photos, except for one of her in front of a log cabin, her arms around the neck of a large black lab. At first Tressa thought it was their family dog, Cocoa, but when she saw the caption of that photo, she then went back to read the others as well:

At home with Daisy.

On Paul's sailboat, Lake Ontario.

Wedding day: Paul with his three brothers and nephew.

Thirty-fifth birthday at Ft. Lauderdale: Paul, Sarah, Jack, Liza.

In that last picture, she stood on a beach, wearing a two-piece bathing suit. Again, Tressa was struck by what was missing as she looked at her perfectly smooth and untouched abdomen. No stretch marks. In reality, Tressa had developed such extreme stretch marks from both pregnancies that she had not worn a bikini since she was nineteen years old.

So, this was the alternate reality she would create for herself by altering the events of that fateful night in January of 1980: no children. No Ellis and no Kassie. There was no Daniel either, but in that moment, Tressa was painfully aware that this did not afflict her nearly as deeply as her missing children did. Who was this Paul? She did not recognize him, Sarah, Jack, or any of the other assumed friends listed in the photos. The only familiar face had been her sister, Liza. Tressa reclined slightly in the chair and shook her head.

So this is my life now? All because I did not go home with Daniel that first night?

The screen again flashed the message from earlier in the day, asking if she wanted more time. No, she did not need to look at these photos anymore. Just like the photo of Ellis on the unknown street corner that she did not recognize, this was not real. This was not her life. An emptiness engulfed her and she felt a chill. She reached down to the floor. Her socks were still there and she pulled them back on. She tried to remember what she was supposed to do to get out of this. Green button? Red button? She could not remember. She only knew that pressing the two simultaneously would lock in this life, this so-called alternate reality, and she did not want that. It seemed to make sense that if she was going to move forward she needed to press the green button. She did so, again with her left hand and the machine flashed a message warning her:

> SIDEBARS ARE CURRENTLY BEING VIEWED. TO SELECT NEXT TIME SEQUENCE PRESS THE GREEN BUTTON WITH RIGHT HAND.

Tressa obediently did as she was told, and the same set of calendars that she had seen before her last journey popped up.

What do I want to do here, ultimately?

She asked herself, fully understanding the rules of this metaphysical game by now. She did not have to ask herself what she wanted, that was clear. She wanted Ellis and Kassie. Without them, her body might as well drift indefinitely through time and space. It was not that her life or her identity were solely defined by motherhood. Recently, this reality had become all the more inescapable, as her children no longer seemed to need her. Nevertheless, without her son and her daughter, Tressa saw her life as a colorless and joyless void. How could she get Ellis back? That was what she needed to figure out. She said it out loud, and found the answer in her particular word order:

How do I get back to Ellis? Of course! I need to go back to that day and all of the hours leading up to his disappearance.

This was also a date she remembered all too well. In fact, Tressa was convinced it would burn in her soul for the rest of her life. Tuesday, November 10, 1998. She repeated the same actions from before, scrolling to land on the year, the month, and the day. She did not know what time she should select, but was mindful that she only had three days total for this journey so she would have to choose wisely. She decided to land on dinnertime the day before. Maybe talking to Ellis the evening before he disappeared would be an important first step. She tried to remember: had they all sat down together for dinner that evening? That had become exceedingly rare in the past few years. She closed her eyes. So much of that time was burned in memory, but most of that was from the days following Ellis's disappearance. She remembered that when she went through his room that Tuesday after work – frantically, disbelieving that things were really as they seemed – there had been a plate of half-eaten pizza on Ellis's desk. She remembered clearly now. She had ordered pizza that night, feeling particularly exhausted after a tough and unsatisfying day of pointless meetings with passive-aggressive colleagues and pontificating superiors. Kassie and Daniel had theirs in front of the TV, she had taken hers to her study, and Ellis had taken his plate of pizza and bottle of tea to his room. She could kick herself now. Why did she leave him alone? She should have insisted they sit together every night at that kitchen table, all four of them, and talk like they used to. She could hear Liza's voice in her head at that moment:

You have to forgive yourself. He was not a toddler in your care, but a young man. You could not watch him every second.

The hell I can't! Tressa decided. She selected the date and was about to lock in her choice when she decided to bring her trench coat and purse this time. She put on the coat, slipped the reservation/portal pod into her back pocket, and pulled her purse over her shoulder, holding on firmly with her free hand. She locked in 19:00 as the time and then pressed the red and green buttons simultaneously. She then remembered at the last moment to press her forehead to the bar.

A blinding flash of light immediately followed and Tressa found herself on all fours, staring at the Berber carpet in her bedroom back home. For a moment, as she was faced with familiar surroundings, smells and sounds, Tressa wondered if everything that had happened that day, or even that week had been a dream. She did not, however, waste too much time on this thought. In a flash, she had dropped her purse and was on her feet, running down the hall to Ellis's room, which immediately provided her with abundant sensory confirmations that he was there. The Foo Fighters' "Everlong" pulsated loudly through his door. But, there was more than just noise. That room, which had remained clean, sterile, and devoid of life for more than a year, now triggered an olfactory overdrive: aromas of pizza, Old Spice deodorant, and Downy fabric softener from his freshly washed bedding wafted through the door. More importantly, Tressa recognized that distinct scent that Ellis had, somewhat reminiscent of eucalyptus; the kind of thing only a mother could identify. She turned the knob slowly, almost afraid of what she might, or might not find, beyond that door.

She opened it, and there he was, sitting at his desk and looking at her with a confused expression. Tressa had a fleeting thought that she should control herself, but she could barely restrain her emotions. She walked over to Ellis, wrapped her arms around him and kissed him on top of his head. She drank in the scent of his hair as she had when he was a baby. A knot formed in her throat and tears were already streaming down her cheek when Ellis pulled back and looked at her.

"Mom, are you OK?"

Tressa summoned her courage and restraint. She cleared her throat. What could she say?

"I'm fine, sweetie. I just came in to see if maybe you wanted to watch a movie with me tonight."

"I think Dad and Kassie are watching something already in the living room."

"Yes, well, I thought we could watch something in the study."

"Like what?"

"Whatever you want. We could go to the video store together and pick something up."

"Alright...sure. If you want to."

"I'll just get my purse and meet you in the car."

Tressa waited in the car in the garage for Ellis for what felt like an eternity. She started to worry and looked at her watch. It had only been about three minutes. Still, she felt, as insane as it was, she should not let Ellis out of her sight. How long could she keep this up? She would only be "there" for three days; that was what the machine had informed her. Could she justify hovering over him, watching his every move for three days? She was certainly going to try. Tressa hoped that she could talk to Ellis; talk in a way that she had before he disappeared. Without being too probing, or too aggressive, she wanted to ask him as much as she could. How was he feeling? Was he going stir crazy at home? Did he want to invite some friends to come with them on their ski holiday planned for that Thanksgiving?

When Ellis did finally get in the car, clicked his seatbelt into place and slumped slightly in his seat, Tressa looked at him and felt tongue-tied. She realized now why she had virtually stopped talking to Ellis once his crisis hit. It was as though she did not know *this* Ellis: he lacked affect, energy, and enthusiasm. He never smiled, and barely said two words unless it was in response to someone's question to him. Also, she remembered too clearly, negotiating a conversation with Ellis post-breakdown had been like navigating a field covered with landmines. Asking him what he did that day would be like a knife jab since Ellis spent every day just filling the hours until he went to sleep. Mentioning his friends was also painful: they were away at school and had, for the most part, moved on with their lives. If she or Daniel brought up the future, Ellis felt cornered and answered defensively that he was "working on it." So, during that period, Tressa had tried to bring up banal, irrelevant subjects just to keep some kind of dialogue going. This was what she resorted to now, using the song on the radio as a platform for their conversation. It was "Dream On," by Aerosmith. Tressa asked her son if he liked these old rock songs.

"They're alright."

Tressa persevered.

"I have a special attachment to this song. I consider it my induction to popular music."

Ellis cast a sidelong glance at his mother but did not say anything.

"I was about thirteen when I first heard it. I was with Liza on a field trip. There was some delay before we left, and the bus driver left his radio on. That song came on, and I was so moved. It was like a transformative experience. I had never heard any piece of music that was so exciting or so powerful." Tressa stopped for moment, wondering why she was being so effusive with Ellis when their usual dynamic was, or had been, one of cautious restraint. She was aware that she was trying with great difficulty to keep her overflowing emotions at seeing her lost son again in check. In an effort to mitigate the emotional level she added,

"I know, it's silly, but you have to understand, Ellis, that Liza and I were very sheltered as children when it came to pop culture."

She was not completely certain, but she thought she heard a harmonizing *mmm-hmm* from Ellis in agreement with her statement. Ellis had spent many weekends and entire weeks in the summer with his maternal grandparents and very little had changed. He and Kassie usually came back from these trips starved for the television programs and popular music their grandparents shunned.

"Is Aerosmith still popular? I mean, do you or your friends ever listen to them?"

"Yeah, some of my friends do, but it's mostly the newer stuff."

"There's new stuff?"

"Yeah, you know, 'Janie's Got a Gun,' 'Rag Doll'."

Tressa did not recognize the songs Ellis mentioned. She had not kept up with much in the way of 'new' music since the early 1980s.

"Maybe you can play those songs for me some time."

"I don't have any of them. I don't really like any of the new stuff. I think the older stuff is actually much better."

Tressa smiled, feeling triumphant at this miniscule victory of keeping Ellis talking. True, he was hardly baring his soul, but still, he was going beyond the perfunctory *yes* or *no*.

She was able to keep this conversational thread in motion until they returned home from the video store. After Tressa had suggested about fifteen titles that met with her son's lukewarm reception, Ellis had finally agreed to the Marx Brothers' *Animal Crackers*. Tressa was relieved. She had steeled herself to watch whatever Ellis might choose, even if it was some awful, generationally unrelatable comedy or violent film. Even though Ellis did not seem overly excited about this film choice, it warmed Tressa's heart to see that they still had this connection.

She had always referred to her son as an "old soul," because he could be easily swayed by nostalgia, and had a penchant for anything 'old timey,' as he used to call it when he was still in elementary school. This included films from the 1930s through the 50s, old music, even old appliances and first edition books that he hunted down at garage sales and purchased for his personal collection – at least before his depression had gotten the better of him.

Tressa went into the kitchen and cast a glance towards the living room couch where Daniel and Kassie were still watching a movie, an action-thriller starring Tommy Lee Jones, Wesley Snipes and Robert Downey Jr. Tressa walked over and picked up the video case, reading the title, *U.S. Marshalls.* She pretended to look on for a few minutes with interest, but neither her husband nor her daughter looked away from the screen, so her effort was in vain. She gave Kassie a kiss on the top of her head and her daughter reciprocated by reaching up and patting her mother on the back of her neck. Kassie's eyes never left the screen, nor did Daniel's, so Tressa walked back to the kitchen.

She rooted around in the pantry until she found the last bag of movie style popcorn and tossed it in the microwave. The smell of salt and butter, which she was sure was most likely hydrogenated oil laden with artificial ingredients, was strangely soothing to her in that moment. She pulled the bag out right before the machine beeped, grabbed a couple of *Snapples*, and joined Ellis in the study where the movie was already cued up to begin.

To her immense relief and satisfaction, Ellis did laugh during the film, something of which she had thought he was no longer capable. He ate very little of the popcorn, but drank his entire bottle of tea and went back to the fridge for nother. When the movie ended, Tressa felt a wave of panic wash over her. What ould she do to make sure he would not disappear that night, short of keeping vigil outside of Ellis's room? She suggested another film, a Laurel and Hardy festival that he had recorded on video from the Cable movie channel a few months earlier. Ellis lid not seem overly excited at the idea, but agreed in a lackluster tone to join her. It occurred to Tressa that her son might have been humoring his poor, pathetic nother in that moment. She did not care. She was going to hold onto him as long as he could.

It turned out to be not that long.

Tressa woke hours later to the sound of static from the TV. She was stretched out on the futon couch, where she had been watching the Laurel and Hardy marathon, covered with a light throw that she kept in the study. Ellis had been watching the films from her office chair, but it was now empty. She realized that Ellis must have covered her with the blanket and left once she had fallen asleep.

Tressa leapt from the couch and tore up the stairs. There was only a sliver of light coming in from the bedroom blinds as she passed Kassie's open room first and saw that she was asleep in her bed. Ellis's door was closed. Tressa held her breath and turned the knob. It did not open. She knocked on the door. Tentatively at first, then more urgently. Before she knew it, she was in full-blown panic mode. She was kicking the door, pounding on it, screaming Ellis's name. A splinter of wood broke loose from one of the bottom panels of the door. Daniel came rushing from their bedroom wearing only his trademark pajama bottoms. He ran his palms over his eyes and asked Tressa in a loud whisper,

"What the hell is going on?"

"It's Ellis! He's in trouble, I just know it, and he's not answering his door."

Daniel repeated Tressa's same actions of moments earlier, first knocking, then calling, then pounding, finally screaming.

After a minute or so, Daniel went downstairs and came back with a small Allen wrench. He unlocked Ellis's door and the two charged into their son's room.

This time was not like the last time (*the real time?*) that Ellis had disappeared. The room was not completely empty, but Ellis was not there either. Tressa looked around and was able to surmise that Ellis had taken a backpack and just a few belongings. So many of the things he prized, however, were still there: his shelf of first edition volumes, his 1950's era phonograph, his box of old Superman comics, and his crate full of old cameras. Not sure of what she was looking for, she rummaged through the box of cameras: a Kodak brownie, a Boy Scout folding camera, a 1949 Leica IIIC, and an Olympus Auto Bellows. She realized that although Ellis had shown these acquisitions to her and Daniel, she could not be entirely sure if any were missing. All she did know was that when Ellis had gone the last time, he had taken all of these things with him. Daniel ran down the stairs and checked the garage. Ellis's car was gone.

"Maybe I didn't travel back early enough?"

"What did you say?"

Daniel asked Tressa in response to her inner monologue, which she had apparently voiced aloud. Tressa wished so desperately that she could tell Daniel what this point in time represented: where she had actually been, how she had come back, but how, despite her best efforts, she had not even managed to stall the departure of their son.

Instead, she just shook her head, tears burning her cheeks, spilling into her mouth, onto her neck. Daniel reached over and pulled her to him. Not mechanically, but tenderly. It was a tenderness she had forgotten was possible with her husband.

"I'm sure he's just gone to a friend's house or something. Don't worry, baby."

Tressa sank into Daniel's chest, gripped his bare shoulder blades with her fingers and sobbed uncontrollably. It was the most she had cried, she realized, since Ellis's initial disappearance in the real world.

Which one of these is the real world, anyway?

In that moment, she could not distinguish reality from illusion, or more aptly, from this nightmare. In either scenario, her son was gone, and she was powerless to change it.

Daniel whispered hushing sounds and called her *baby*, and *darling*, and all of the pet names she had long ago stopped responding to, and which at some point he had stopped calling her. Now, on this transcendental plane, Tressa was startled to discover how effective her husband's comforting was.

"Why don't you go lie down for a few minutes and I'll put the coffee on. If Ellis doesn't come back in a few hours, we can make some phone calls."

Again Tressa wanted to protest, to divulge what Ellis's absence really meant, and to explain to Daniel how she had come to possess this prescient knowledge. Instead, she obediently went to their room, receiving a warm and loving kiss from Daniel before he went downstairs to make the coffee.

Tressa lay on her side, emotionally bereft, and physically spent. She could not go through all of this again. Not even for three more days. Furthermore, she could not see the point. What new leads could she possibly unearth? Fleetingly, she contemplated being able to transport herself to Nevada at the precise moment Ellis had sold the car. Could she rely on that? After all, the sequence of events had changed slightly this time. Undoubtedly, she had upset something in the universe. This time Ellis disappeared hours earlier than he had in the real world, and with only a fraction of his possessions. Tressa wondered what possible side effects might result from this alternate reality. She felt the fatigue and feverish chills return and she pulled the heavy comforter up to her chin and slipped effortlessly into a deep sleep.

6

Tressa opened her eyes. Before her lay an expansive and glimmering body of water extending, it appeared, endlessly beyond the horizon. An abundance of red and white beach umbrellas and blue chaise lounges gave her the impression of a Mediterranean resort. She did not process that this was a dream, but in her dormant state of consciousness, she also did not remember the time traveling, or the fact that Ellis had disappeared. All she knew was that she was standing a good distance from the shoreline, where she could see Daniel, Kassie and Ellis. The sight of her children filled her with a buoyancy that made her quicken her pace. When she reached them, she saw that they were building a sand castle. Daniel was kneeling next to Kassie. The Kassie that she saw in her dream was the same Kassie that she had seen right before she had left for Boston: tall, athletic, with three earrings in one ear, her only outward sign of adolescent rebellion. Her long legs were outstretched on the sand, and she was only half-heartedly contributing to the architectural masterpiece, as

hough she was really just humoring her dad. Daniel, by contrast, was putting his
eart and soul into the project as he always had when it came to doing things with
he children. He had created support beams for the castle, using driftwood and
ocks, and was currently digging a moat that was truly an impressive feat of
ngineering. Tressa complimented them on their work of art, and then asked them,

Where's Ellis?

Daniel and Kassie shrugged and Tressa scanned the shoreline for her son. Only
noments earlier, Ellis had been kneeling beside his sister, contributing water to the
tructure that he had collected in his beach pail.

Tressa spotted the bright red pail that now lay on the shoreline, and then
Ellis, who was swimming towards a rock formation maybe twenty-five feet out.
Jnlike the dream-state version of Kassie, the Ellis that Tressa saw was younger, not
quite a teen, maybe twelve or so, still bearing his pre-pubescent chubbiness around
he face. Tressa did not question the funny age disparity between older brother and
younger sister that was now reversed in an exaggerated way. Instead, she just stood
here and watched her boy as he swam.

The water was starting to get a little rough, but Ellis had been a strong
swimmer from the age of five, and Tressa knew he would not venture out too far.
Suddenly, however, she could tell that something was very wrong. Although he had
not gone out that far, Ellis was now clearly struggling. He was being pulled out

further by what must have been an undercurrent or a riptide of some sort. Tressa could not hear him, but she could see the urgency in her child's face. Never having been much of a swimmer herself, she screamed for Daniel, who was suddenly nowhere to be found. The beach was eerily empty, stripped of all people as well as the umbrellas and beach chairs. Sensing the imminent danger, Tressa quickly kicked off her shoes so that she could swim out to Ellis. She looked once more for Daniel before heading for the water, and then, as is the nature of dreams, suddenly Tressa was standing next to Rico Suarez, her would-be love interest. Rico had grabbed her by the forearms and was restraining her. He was telling her that it was *too late*:

You cannot give up your life for Ellis. You have to let him go. He is gone.

Tressa pried herself away from Rico, but then collapsed to her knees sobbing as she lost sight of the shoreline and the water altogether.

7

Daniel would not have let Ellis go. Daniel would have saved him.

This was Tressa's thought in the dream, but she also voiced it aloud when she woke up abruptly, only ten minutes or so after she had drifted off. She had been awakened by the *Underground* reservation device, still in her back pocket, which had started humming and vibrating. Tressa pulled it out, and waited for the flash of lights and predictable message to pop up, as though she had done this a hundred times before. Once again, the small pod informed her of the nearest portal; a phone booth at an address that she vaguely recognized as being on the outskirts of downtown, 512 North Harrington Street. Tressa mechanically slid off the bed, and dragged herself downstairs, slipping through the study to the hall next to the garage to avoid Daniel's questions. He heard her moving in the other room and called out:

"The coffee's ready, honey – do you want me to make some toast?"

Tressa answered quickly as she moved, not wanting to linger a moment longer than she had to:

"I think I need a sugar fix. I'm going to run out for donuts. I'll be right back."

"Are you sure? Do you want me to go with you?"

"No need. Be back in a flash."

Tressa did not hesitate, and within seconds, she was in the garage starting the car. As she backed out of her driveway, she was suddenly overcome with an almost paralyzing feeling of heaviness and despair. She had been through all of this before – why did the pain feel so much deeper now?

Tressa set out down her street realizing that she was not entirely sure how to get to North Harrington. She felt the oppressive heat radiating again from her body, and rolled down the windows. A recent rain had made the streets slick, and the few cars and buses made whooshing sounds as they went by. The sky had a grey cast to it, and Tressa realized she still had no idea what time it was. She decided that she would head downtown and ask for directions to North Harrington at the nearest gas station. After driving for about twelve minutes, she spotted a Shell looming a few blocks over. She had to laugh as she turned onto the street realizing that not only was she on North Harrington, but the address, 512, was that of the Shell station itself. It was an older station that looked as though it had not been emodeled in the last two decades.

Tressa pulled in reluctantly, noticing that the station was still closed and here was no sign of life anywhere. On the opposite side of the station, away from he pumps and closer to the street, stood a lone phone booth, the old-fashioned, full-cabin style that had been replaced in most places by the smaller, boxier, open units on pedestals. Miraculously, most of the Plexiglas panels remained on this booth, although several layers of street art, done up in mostly black spray paint, covered the remaining panes so that one could barely see inside, or out. Tressa turned off the car and locked it, wondering for a brief moment that if she really did transport from this time and place, what would happen to her car? Would the Tressa from 1998 still be there and return home with donuts? Or, would Kassie and Daniel suddenly find themselves puzzled over her disappearance as well? She worried if this sidebar could erase her from their lives indefinitely and cause even more destructive ripples in her family's life. Still, she felt she had to keep moving; she had to keep trying until she found Ellis.

Tressa stepped into the phone booth and had to step back out to suppress her gag reflex. The stench that had met her once inside the booth was overpowering: urine, sweat, tobacco, and other unmentionable odors. Tressa reached into her purse and pulled out a tissue. She sprayed it with *Casmir*, her favorite vanilla and cloves perfume that she carried with her everywhere. Tressa had always had a strong sense of smell, and was easily nauseated by even milder malodorous encounters in public spaces. What she encountered in that phone booth would take a great deal of mind control and holding her breath. She breathed in the fresh outdoor air, held the scented tissue to her face, and stepped back into the alleged portal. The device in her pocket vibrated, and Tressa read the message instructing her to wait for a phone call. In that moment, the phone rang, and Tressa was faced with a choice. Take a chance that the phone receiver was hygienic enough to touch with her bare hand, or relinquish her scent guard and use the tissue to pick up the phone. She decided neither would do and fished around in her purse with her left hand for another tissue while still holding the scented one to her face with her right. She found the same café napkin and used that to grab the receiver, holding it as far away from her face as possible, while still being able to hear any message the machine might convey. She heard nothing at first, and uttered a tentative, *Hello*? Once again, as in the Student Union photo booth, she was met with the sound of a dial-up modem and a blinding white light that filled the odiferous cabin.

In what felt like no passage of time at all, Tressa found herself standing a few feet away from the microfilm machine, and just like last time, the sounds, light and scents indicated that the coffee shop and bookstore were still in full swing.

She sat down at the microfilm machine, tapped the top of it, and the machine whirred to life, flashing the same message she had seen earlier:

PRESS GREEN BUTTON WITH LEFT HAND TO

SEE POSSIBLE SIDEBARS OF LAST TRAVEL

SEQUENCE. PRESS RED BUTTON FOR HELP. PRESS RED AND GREEN BUTTON TO LOCK IN CHOICE. PRESS GREEN BUTTON WITH RIGHT HAND TO SELECT NEXT TRAVEL SEQUENCE.

Tressa pressed the green button eagerly; sweat was now running down her neck and back, pure adrenaline pushing her on. There was no time to factor in fear, anticipation, or any emotions. She felt an urgency she had not yet felt up to this point, but she did not stop to contemplate what that meant.

The screen filled with photographic images and brief captions as it had the last time, and Tressa was puzzled for a moment since she recognized them as representing various situations from the past year. Had this trip not altered anything?

Then she saw it, a grainy, black and white image that looked like a newspaper photo. She zoomed in and realized that it was, in fact, a newspaper photo. The caption underneath was lettered in newspaper font, and Tressa had to read it three times before it sunk in.

Kassie Stevens, shown next to her mother, Tressa Novak, places a new wreath on the roadside shoulder where her brother Ellis was killed by a drunk driver in the early morning hours of November 10, 1998. Tressa Novak and her husband Daniel Stevens have been petitioning local authorities for the past year to allow roadside memorials that are banned under county littering

ordinances.

What happened next was as involuntary as the sensation when her body had been catapulted through time and space. Tressa lunged sideways, just catching the wastebasket next to the desk as she emptied the contents of her stomach, which contained, to her surprise, a mixture of Jack Daniels and Coke, as well as peach-flavored iced tea and artificially flavored popcorn. If she really did consume those things during those ethereal journeys, did that mean that the newspaper article could be true? Had she actually worsened Ellis's fate by going back early? It was unthinkable. This too, she decided, was an alternate reality. She stood up, feeling dizzy and queasy and made her way back to the desk chair. She folded over the cuff of her long-sleeved t-shirt and wiped her mouth with the inside of it. For the first time in what felt like hours, she felt thirsty and an urgent need to pee. She could not, however, afford to take any chances by waiting. She had to cancel or nullify this alternate reality immediately. Moving with a deftness and an almost controlled deliberation that surprised her, Tressa pressed the green button with her right index finger. As she did so, she was vaguely aware of the wedding ring that had, at some point, reappeared on her left hand. She then went through the assortment of dates, days, and times, having already decided that she had to go back to Ellis's childhood this time and try to root out the source of this problem. Still fresh in her mind was the dream she had had, strangely enough, during her last time travel sequence. Had there been a message hidden in that dream? What was the symbolism of Ellis being swept off to sea? In the dream, Ellis appeared to be twelve years old. Did that mean anything? She had to choose the next date she traveled to wisely since she would only be permitted three days total. She still needed to ascertain where exactly the problems began for Ellis. After seeing that newspaper headline, Tressa was sure that she not only had to prevent Ellis from leaving on November 10, 1998, but that she had to avert his entire self-destructive crash that year.

8

Tressa chose a date in October of 1992, a few days before Ellis turned twelve. Besides the potential omen embedded in her dream, reaching Ellis when he was on the cusp of adolescence seemed to be the best tactical move at that point. She pressed the green and red buttons and as she applied her forehead to the bar above, she noticed for the first time that music was playing in the store. *Heaven* by the Psychedelic Furs came on just seconds before Tressa was launched into the blinding white light.

This time, however, rather than an instantaneous landing in the next temporal dimension, she found herself in what felt like a glass vestibule, or a revolving door. The bright light had only dimmed slightly, and she had to squint, trying to get her bearings as one does in a dark room before their eyes adjust to their compromised vision. She reached out to see if she could open a door, or make out the form of something, but her hand met with instant resistance, as though she were nside a tautly wrapped plastic bubble. She closed her eyes and tried to regulate her breathing. Even under the best of circumstances, Tressa was prone to panic attacks. A few years earlier, when she hit her head in a clumsy fall down the back patio steps, her doctor had ordered an MRI. The first attempt at the procedure had to be aborted after less than two minutes had passed. Once inside the narrow, magnetic chamber, Tressa felt suddenly unable to breathe. The second attempt was successful only because her doctor had pre-medicated her with a prescription tranquilizer.

Now, in this unknown, over-illuminated sphere, with no anchors, no bearings, and, at this point, no control over her movement, it did not take long for a feeling of anxiety to wash over her. As Tressa felt her heart rate accelerate, she forced herself to open her eyes again and take stock of her surroundings. She knew if she could remain calm, relatively speaking, she could most likely find a way out.

No breathing exercises, or meditation, however, could have prepared her for what she saw next. Beyond the bubble in which she was entombed, at least for the moment, there was another bubble. The same white light that filled her chamber surrounded the space between her and the other bubble. Tressa squinted and could see people moving around inside it. She pushed her body hard towards the flexible wall in front of her, and found that by kneading it, she could move it, and herself, closer to the other bubble. It felt a bit like a beanbag, and just as hard to manipulate. Eventually she found herself facing the other bubble, looking in. It was considerably darker in this bubble, but she saw a room that she recognized as her parents' old kitchen in the house where she had grown up. In reality, they had just sold that house about three years ago, to move into a condominium in Hilton Head. Seated at the counter that Tressa recognized all too well, was a young boy stirring something in a large bowl. He looked up, but even before he did so, she recognized his movements. It was Ellis. Tressa's mother was standing close by, giving him instructions, or so it would appear. In fact, Tressa could not hear anything outside her bubble; she could only see their facial expressions and their mouths moving. Tressa watched this scene for quite a while, marveling at her son's youthful energy and boundless joy. This was the Ellis she remembered. She smiled as she admired his innocent, almost goofy quality as he helped his grandmother in the kitchen. Tressa was also struck by how much younger and more agile her mother seemed to be only seven years earlier. After more stirring, and the greasing and flouring of pans, Tressa realized that her mother and Ellis were making his birthday cake. She remembered that Ellis celebrated his twelfth birthday at his grandparents', having spent the previous Friday night there with Kassie as well. Later that day, she and Daniel came over with gifts. No sooner had she recalled that detail that she saw a sight that most closely resembled a home movie: she watched herself walk into the kitchen with Daniel; she was carrying the gifts, Daniel had a stack of pizzas. A young Kassie, her hair pulled back in a bouncy ponytail, walked in at that moment and gave her dad a hug. When no one was looking, she slid her finger along the rim of the mixing bowl to taste the cake batter. Tressa watched from her bubble as Kassie then slipped off into the other room, which the younger Tressa did not seem o notice. Daniel, meanwhile, was sitting at the kitchen table talking to Tressa's dad who had just walked in. Tressa watched her seven-years-younger self interact with Ellis: she wrapped herself around him in a big bear hug, to which he responded by rolling his eyes in embarrassment. Tressa took the stool next to Ellis at the counter and talked to him, and he seemed happy to talk to her. After a few minutes, the younger Tressa cocked her head slightly and mouthed something to her mother who was still puttering in the kitchen. Tressa could not read the lips of her younger self, but did not need to. She could remember clearly what she had told her mother; she was identifying the piano piece that Kassie was playing from the other room. She felt a heaviness as she recalled this memory; it was tinged with sadness for her. On the trip back home that night, Kassie had asked her parents why nobody had paid attention to her that day. Daniel answered that he was sorry, it certainly was not intentional; it was Ellis's birthday so he naturally would be the center of attention. Despite Daniel's attempt to justify their apparent slight, Kassie started to cry:

"I played *Hungarian Rhapsody* perfectly, and no one even came in the living room to listen to me."

Tressa remembered vividly the pain in her daughter's voice. Watching this scene now she was struck by how little, in fact, she seemed to interact with Kassie. Surely, this must be an anomalous situation. It had to have been as Daniel had explained: it was Ellis's birthday, and Ellis was naturally the focus of everyone's attention. In her heart, however, Tressa could not accept this explanation. She wished she could manipulate the scene she was watching with a remote control so she could scan the sequence of events and determine if she had indeed neglected Kassie for that entire evening. She did not want to endure watching it unfold in real time; the pain was too great. Tressa watched for about twenty more minutes. At a certain point, Kassie returned to the kitchen and Tressa said something to her with a smile. If she remembered correctly, she had praised her daughter on how well she had executed that piece. But she said all this without leaving her stool, without leaving her son's side.

How could I have missed this?

Tressa spoke aloud, chiding herself harshly. All this time, since Ellis's disappearance, she had convinced herself that somehow she had not paid enough attention to her son, that she had failed him somehow. In that collection of brief moments that spanned no more than a half an hour, Tressa witnessed what she knew was representative of her dynamic with Ellis. The closeness and the unwavering affection. A bond she took for granted that she also shared with her daughter but apparently did not. At least not on the same level as she shared it with Ellis.

Tressa then remembered a book she had started to read a few months after Ellis was born called *The Holding Continuum.* It was a book extolling Rudolf Steiner's philosophy on raising children. Tressa's friend Lacey, a devout follower and supporter of the anthroposophist movement, had lent her the book to reassure her that the constant attention and physical contact Tressa maintained with her newborn – including co-sleeping, carrying him in a baby sling instead of a stroller, and so on, was not only natural, but healthy. Tressa found the book, as well as the movement in general, too doctrinaire and steeped in rituals for her taste. However, the basic premise was that by consistently maintaining that physical closeness – by constantly holding your baby, you actually fostered a strong sense of security that in turn enhanced the child's sense of self and identity. She was not sure what to make of all of this now, given Ellis's abrupt departure from his home and his family. Had she, in fact, smothered him? Did she drive him away? And what about Kassie, who seemed fine? More than fine, in fact. It was Kassie who had been the glue that held the remnants of their family together since Ellis had left. Was she really suffering on the inside? Tressa made a mental note, more like a pledge, to talk to her daughter at length when she made it back home. If she ever made it back home.

Tressa was suddenly overcome by a weariness that she had not felt since her first trip through the time portal. She wanted to sit down, but was afraid she might not be able to get back up into a standing position once she sat on the almost gelatinous floor of this strange, light filled-orb. In that moment, Tressa remembered the reservation device in her back pocket. Up until now, it had notified her when she had changed the sequence of events, and had prompted her to find the nearest portal back. She wondered if she could not just initiate the transmission of information herself. Could she proactively get the device to transport her back?

She was beginning to feel claustrophobic again and felt the simultaneous buildup of nausea and a clammy dizziness start to take over. She had to get out of this space at all costs. Tressa pulled the device out of her back pocket and shook it trying to elicit some sort of response. When the blank screen still did not show any sign of life, Tressa tapped it. First, with an almost detached air of curiosity, and then with an increasing sense of almost manic urgency. At that moment, the light outside her chamber dimmed, and Tressa felt a subtle but distinct movement. It was somewhat like traveling in an airplane with no actual turbulence, but with enough vibrations to convey the sensation of moving. She held her arms out at her sides, raised slightly, as though to ensure she would maintain a sense of balance and equilibrium. The spongy floor beneath her developed a momentum of soft, slow rippling. The ripples all seemed to be moving in a forward direction, so Tressa decided that must be where she was heading – whatever *forward* meant at this point. There was no loud, audible noise, but Tressa felt a pounding and heard a slight whooshing in her ears. Then, the dimmed light outside the bubble went out completely, and the incandescent light that surrounded her diminished. The ripples beneath her feet, harder to see without the bright light, seemed to be slowing down too. Then there was complete darkness, and a rush of cold air washed over her.

Tressa closed her eyes instinctively and again concentrated on her breathing. When she finally opened them, the spongy bubble was gone. She was standing in her stocking feet on the floor of the bookstore, inches away from the ack fire door. Tressa looked around for her shoes and realized she must have left hem, or lost them involuntarily, near the microfilm machine. Or, at least that was what she hoped. It would be a long trip back to her aunt's in this weather with no hoes. Suddenly, a wave of panic washed over her as she realized that she was also nissing her purse. *Did I even have it with me in that mystical sphere?* The panic, fatigue, nd nausea all welled up in her in that moment, and Tressa felt her airways constricting. She lunged towards the *Exit* sign, pressed down on the aluminum bar nd forced the old, heavy door open. She hurled herself outside, not giving any egard to the sign posted next to the door warning her about the Fire Alarm.

9

Despite the warning, the fire alarm did not sound when Tressa opened the emergency door. Tressa found herself on the sidewalk, a mingling of odors–dry rot from the old door, automobile exhaust, and the sour, fetid odor of garbage – welcoming her to the outside. Beyond the smells, the overwhelming and startling sensation was the light and the warmth. The icy rain and grey skies she had encountered earlier that day had melted into what felt like a balmy summer day. The light was so intense Tressa had to squint to evaluate her surroundings. Despite the muggy and malodorous atmospheric conditions, the fresh air felt good, and Tressa inhaled deeply. She leaned forward slightly, her hands on her thighs just above her knees as she did so, shaking off the last feelings of vertigo and nausea.

As she straightened herself upright, an odd feeling crept over her that something was familiar about this place. Not just this patch of sidewalk, this corner of the building that housed the bookstore, but something she could not put her finger on. She might have dismissed it as a sense of déjà vu, had she not clearly recognized something. It hit her in approximately the same moment she became aware of people passing her in unseasonable clothing: polo shirts, shorts, skirts, and other summer clothes. That microfilm image Tressa had seen before she started any of these journeys, the one of Ellis, standing on what had been an unrecognizable street corner, bathed in the glow of the high summer sun, had been taken here, in this spot. The quality and abundance of sunlight in that photo, coupled with the knowledge that Ellis had headed West when he disappeared, had led Tressa to conclude erroneously that the photo had been taken in some California city or town.

Ellis was here in Boston? When?

Clearly, Tressa had not been transported back to December of 1999. She caught a few sidelong glances directed at her standing there in the sweltering heat dressed in jeans, a heavy sweater, thick socks, and no shoes. Tressa pulled her sweater off as the heat became increasingly unbearable, and tied it around her waist. She could not even begin to wonder what had brought Ellis to Boston, or when he might have been here. She decided to head back to the store, to the machine, in the hopes that she would make it back to a point in time that she could at least recognize or navigate, even if she could not control it. She was growing increasingly fearful that she would not ever make it back, but would be stuck in what she could only define as some sort of time warp. As she turned around to head for the fire exit, Tressa felt a tap on her shoulder. She wheeled around and saw the same vaguely familiar visage captured in that eerie photo.

“Ellis?”

Tressa had no sooner voiced this out loud that she collapsed into an involuntary deluge of tears. She grabbed Ellis by the shoulders and pulled him close, hugging him. He hugged her back, patting her between the shoulder blades in the same way he had when he was a toddler and she would try to soothe him for bedtime, carrying him, patting him on the back. She had always found it so endearing that at such a young age he would reciprocate that gesture. Tressa released him slightly, still holding him by the forearms, and surveyed the face before her. As in the image the machine had shown her, Ellis looked somewhat gaunt and careworn. Upon closer examination however, Tressa realized that it was not lack of health, or a state of trauma that had changed his features so radically, but simply age. She was looking into the eyes of her son who was no longer a teenager, but now at least in his thirties. This time, unlike the other journeys, she had traveled forward, into the future.

“Hey, Mom.”

Ellis said this with a hint of a smile, but mostly with an air of weariness, the heaviness that overtakes people when they have to break bad news. Ellis took her by the arm and led her to the bench at the bus stop. They sat down and Tressa tried to imagine how she would explain to her son what she was doing there in her winter clothes and no shoes, and why, when it was obviously more than ten years later, she had not aged.

"Ellis, I don't know how to tell you this..."

Ellis raised his hand as a sign of gentle protest and said,

"Mom. I know why you're here."

Tressa shot him a puzzled look, but then, like everything else that she had experienced thus far on this odyssey, the unimaginable and seemingly improbable suddenly felt not only comprehensible, but completely within the realm of normalcy.

She nodded, trying to soak it all in, sifting through layers of questions, originating with the most burning question concerning Ellis's disappearance on that grey November day. *Why?*

Oddly enough, however, it was the mature Ellis, sitting next to her at this bus stop that motivated her first question.

"Hang, on Ellis: what are you doing here, now, with me? And how could you possibly know why I am here, or how I got here?" For the first time since her first teleportation to the campus bar in 1980, Tressa was overcome with the feeling that this had to be a dream. Or, given the detail and longevity of this journey, it was more likely a prolonged state of unconsciousness. How could she possibly evaluate the real and unreal when everything seemed so otherworldly? What followed, in Ellis's explanation, did not help to make this distinction any clearer.

"Many years ago..."

Ellis began, and then laughed.

"Well, many years ago for me, but what would be about two and a half years ago to you now, I was messing around at an antique fair – you know the one they always held every year at the State Fairgrounds – looking at old cameras, and I got to talking with a guy who specialized in antiquated photography equipment. He was lamenting the advent of digital cameras, something that had been relatively mass-produced on a commercial level for at least two or three years at that point, but which few of us had ever seen, let alone heard of. This old guy was a bit of a kook; I mean he was a caricature, complete with a long beard and even longer, unkempt hair. But, he knew his trade. Once he realized that I was actually interested in hearing what he had to say, he kept me there for probably close to an hour. He educated me on the subtleties of contrast, the richness of shade and varying degrees of light that you could tweak in a dark room, but that would no longer be possible with digital cameras. For me, the concept of a digital camera was, at that point in my limited frame of reference, just that: a concept. As I think you know, I dabbled in photography, but I didn't develop the film myself. I think I asked dad once if I could take over the garage as a dark room and he shot that idea down. You were also not too thrilled about the prospect of losing a bathroom for that purpose."

Ellis paused and laughed, this time a genuine smile spreading across the fine lines that now defined his face. Tressa smiled too, and Ellis continued.

"Anyway, when I seemed bewildered by what this guy was trying to tell me, he insisted I check out his darkroom and try to develop some film on my own. Which I did, a few times. His darkroom was located at the back of his regular shop. Besides hawking his wares at the Antiques Fair, he also had an established store on Duke Street in Durham. This was around the same time I got my driver's license and the car that Dad and I fixed up, so I used to go there occasionally after school, or on the occasional Saturday. I would help him out in the shop, and instead of paying me, he let me use the darkroom, and provided all the chemicals and paper for me to use. It was then that I truly became aware of what this old character had been rhapsodizing about. By taking control of the whole process, everything from surrounding yourself with the odors of the chemicals you need to mix, to adjusting the aperture; playing with base exposures, dodging and burning, and so forth, the image you end up with becomes so much more than just a photograph. It is art. And, because you have used your hands to create it, it is truly yours. To this day, even when we have the capability to take photos on our phones..."

Ellis paused, noticing his mother's somewhat confused expression, and let this concept sink in,

"I still like to play around in the darkroom. Anyway, on one of these days that I went to his shop – oh, by the way, the guy's name was Loren – Loren was nowhere to be found. The shop was open, and I had waited, expecting him to turn up. After several minutes, I got tired of waiting and just went into the darkroom to experiment with a few of my negatives. When I opened the door to the darkroom I was surprised to find the lights on – Loren always left them off unless one of us were in there and had completed the development process. The second surprising thing I noticed was an old plate camera, the type with the bellows, where the photographer would duck under a cloth, or hood, to take the picture. That particular camera had not been in the shop previously, which was not necessarily unusual. Loren was constantly making new acquisitions of antique equipment. Typically, I might have waited, and asked Loren before trying out any of the new stuff. However, since it was clear that Loren was not there, I gave into my burning curiosity. I started to explore by handling and manipulating every aspect of the camera, then I set up a prop for a still photo: an apple from my lunch that I positioned on a stool. I then stuck my head under the hood, making sure I had a clear view of the subject of the shot, in this case, the apple. I noticed that there was a small mirror above the apple, framed in a weathered old picture frame, and thought it would be a neat effect if I could capture my image, kind of ghost-like, hovering above the apple. Once I was satisfied with the set-up, I decided to try to take the picture. I didn't know if there was film already loaded into the camera, but just decided to squeeze the bulb and see what would happen next. What did happen next I initially interpreted as the camera's flash – all I saw was blinding light – but after the intense burst of luminosity receded, I realized I was no longer in Loren's shop, but in some dark, alley paved with cobblestone. When a horse-drawn carriage almost ran me over, I realized something was really off.

In a nutshell, that was the first of many time travel episodes. Initially, Mom, I was afraid that I was...well, in a word, *tripping*."

Ellis said this last word gingerly, as though he did not want to reopen that wound which for him had healed long ago, but was still relatively fresh for his mom. Ellis's experimentation with drugs had been dismissed as just that by the staff at the hospital treatment center they had checked him into all those years ago. Still, Tressa had worried when Ellis disappeared that his dependency issue had actually been more severe than anyone had realized. Up until now, Tressa had hung on Ellis's every word, too overwhelmed by his presence and by her emotions, to speak. Now she broke her silence and asked the question that had left her with a searing pain ever since that grim November day.

"Is that why you left?"

Ellis shrugged slightly before nodding and then continuing.

"I went on about two more trips, I mean, through time, before I decided I had to leave home. I was so mixed up. I couldn't tell you or dad about these journeys. You never would have believed me. Worse yet, you would most certainly have had me committed again. This time for possibly an indefinite period of time. I just could not have withstood that. I honestly didn't see any other way out."

Tressa shrugged herself this time, but then had to agree with his assessment. Tears started to stream down her cheeks and Ellis put his arm around her and whispered a hushing sound as though she were a little girl. Tressa felt suddenly embarrassed by her son's reaction and her own lack of composure. With tremendous effort, she pulled herself upright and cleared her throat.

"So where *did* you go? And where have you been all these years? Will I get to see you again in the real world? Have you settled into a life somewhere? Are you happy?"

Ellis laughed again, this time somewhat nervously.

"Mom, everything turns out just fine. Yes, I come back. Not as soon as I know you'd hope, but you have to let it go and just wait for me to sort it all out – which I did. Eventually I realized I could do this – the traveling – as a kind of pastime, kind of like my antique collections or photography. So, I continue to go back and visit various points in my past, or in other times in history. I don't, however, travel to points in the future. I've learned the hard way that if you know what is going to happen in your future, you change your behavior, and by so doing may set in action an alternate reality that is much worse than what you would have experienced had you simply left it alone."

Tressa opened her mouth to ask Ellis what had happened on this future trip, arching her eyebrows as she always did when she was concerned, but again, he held up his hand to stop her.

"Don't worry, Mom. Whatever damage I caused I managed to fix for the most part. In the end, it was nothing catastrophic. It's just as well you don't know. However, I wanted to leave you with some scientific proof, or at least supporting data for what's gone on so that you won't doubt yourself when you return to the real world. Most of this is in the article I left in the box of microfilm near the machine at the Underground Traveler's Bookstore that you printed out."

"Quantum theory?"

Tressa remembered the gist of the article very well.

"Yes, I read that article. But how did you know I'd be here, or that I printed out the article?"

"You have to trust me when I tell you, Mom, that I just cannot answer those questions right now. As far as quantum theory, you can read more about it... well, actually some of the best stuff has come out in the past few years. For now, there are plausible theories ranging in time from Einstein's day to the most recent studies. The various hypotheses are nicely summarized in that article I left for you which came out this year. For example, quantum theory explains what I was cautioning against with regards to the future. It's not that the future is fixed. Instead, viewing all matter reduced to electrons or atoms, quantum theory suggests that before they are definitively measured, objects exist simultaneously in many different states. This is called a "superposition." When we measure these objects, a choice is made, or the superposition is "collapsed." In fact, the act of measurement itself, which in the broader context of what we've been talking about, life itself, making definitive choices, determines that choice or that final state. Kind of gives the idea of fate a kick in the pants, eh?"

Tressa shook her head and tried to laugh, but once again, she felt herself succumbing to her fatigue. Ellis continued talking as Tressa took off her heavy socks and placed them next to her on the bus stop bench, trying desperately to cool down.

"There's a whole lot more to it, including all kinds of stuff about the Copenhagen Interpretation and wave function. My favorite nuggets in all this complicated theorizing that even Einstein never embraced are the following: the idea that one particle on one side of the universe can affect another particle without even sending anything tangible from that one segment of the universe to the other. This may sound very New Agey to you, something I know you might be inclined to reject, Mom. However, recently, in maybe 2009 or so, social scientists started getting in on this and have expanded this theory to explain why people with a strong physical, emotional, or biological connection to another person can anticipate, feel, or empathize on an almost palpable level what this other person is feeling, emoting, or even thinking."

"Quantum entanglement. Yes, I found that fascinating."

"Isn't it? So I guess what I'm trying to say is that…"

At this point, Ellis's voice trailed off and he turned away momentarily as though he needed to compose himself before continuing,

"I know you Mom, and I know that you will blame yourself for everything that goes wrong with just about everybody close to you. It's like Catholic guilt to the tenth degree. I'm sure that you have been torturing yourself thinking that my downward spiral and eventual vanishing act was somehow your fault. But, Mom: it wasn't."

Tressa hated herself for crying in that moment. Despite the surreal circumstances, or the fact that her son was now in his thirties, she still felt an obligation to be a stronger, more solid role model for him. Nevertheless, she could not help it. She grabbed Ellis's hand and listened as he continued to grant his absolution.

"No, really Mom. I mean, sure, there were things you and dad did, or didn't do, that pissed me off and some that took me a while to work through, but I know now that you really did the best you could, and that you always put me and Kassie above everything else. A bit too much at times, in fact, at the cost of your marriage. But I've forgiven you, just as I know you will forgive the teen-aged me for causing you so much grief and heartache. In the end, it is your love for me that keeps us connected; it is this bond that essentially facilitated the two of us coming together here, in this moment, from two remote dimensions of the universe."

A thought, or at least an emotion that was not fully formed in a logical way, hit Tressa in that moment and she blurted it out without hesitating:

"Ellis, I just realized: you're a dad, aren't you? No, I know you are; I can see it in your eyes. I can feel it. That's why you can forgive me; you understand…"

Ellis did not answer her question, but a slight and fleeting smile flashed across his face before he spoke:

"Mom, you need to trust me now. You have to go. You have to go back. I don't have time to explain any of the mechanics involved, but let me just say that there are more regimented modes of time travel–like your microfilm machine, photo or telephone booth, and so on – and then there is the mode that brought us here in this moment, which is more like ocean surfing. You have to know when to catch a wave and how long to ride it. If you don't seize the opportunity at the right moment under those circumstances, you can end up either in dangerously choppy waters, or in still, placid, unmoving water. Either way, you may never find your way back to shore. You have to go right now. We'll see each other soon. I promise."

Feeling once again like a little girl, Tressa nodded obediently, although she was not sure why she didn't cling to Ellis, and insist he come back with her regardless of the consequences. Ellis helped her up and embraced her, kissing her on top of her head. Tressa kissed her son on the forehead and both cheeks, as she had when he was little, and hugged him once more before turning to go back to the fire exit. The hot pavement scorched her bare feet, and only as she reached the door to the bookstore did Tressa realize that she had left her socks on the bus stop bench. She turned around and saw Ellis still standing there, striking the same pose, the same exact glance she had seen in that microfilm photo. Tressa thought about making her way back to get her socks when a white-hot blaze of light encircled Ellis. She realized it was the same quality of light she had seen in that microfilm photo that had initially caught her attention. Ellis bent down as though he were retrieving something from under the bench – and then disappeared. Tressa ran over to the bench, cutting her toe on a piece of green glass, but she was no longer aware of either the heat radiating from the city pavement nor any physical pain. Ellis was gone. She was filled with an icy feeling of loneliness. An anxiety attack hit her full force in that moment, complete with heart palpitations. Ellis's words of caution, which he had delivered fervently, even urgently, rang in her ears in that moment and drove her back in the direction of the fire door.

If Tressa could have narrated what happened next – to whom she did not know – she would have described that scene as unfolding in a sort of slow motion. The fire door, which she had flung open and which had, apparently, stayed open during her visit with Ellis, was now closing. There was nobody in sight, and no wind pushing it, so whether it was simply gravity or a paranormal force responsible, Tressa did not know. All she knew was that if that door closed, she might not ever get back. Lacking any concrete explanations, Tressa was propelled purely by her gut instinct. She started to run, and then resorted to hobbling quickly on her now bloody foot, towards the door with the eerie sensation that she would never make it. Time seemed to stand still as she found herself reflecting on her life thus far: on what Ellis had said, on whether or not she could trust his words, and if she could forgive herself for all her failings and shortcomings. As Tressa reached the door, she thought she could hear strains of a tune from *Animal Crackers*, the film she had watched with Ellis the night before his second disappearance, "Hooray for Captain Spaulding…"

10

Tressa just managed to slip her fingers into the doorjamb and push back on the door with her hip as it was closing. Once inside, the door shut behind her with a resounding thud. She no longer could hear the old film melody in her head, and the sounds from the street outside were completely muted. A rush of cold wind whipped around her ankles as Tressa made her way back to the machine. She looked down at her injured foot to inspect the severity of the wound and was stunned to see that there was no blood. She leaned up against a pillar and shifted her weight from one leg to the other as she looked at the bottoms of her feet. There were no cuts, scrapes, or even the grime she would have expected from traversing a city street without shoes or socks. She continued to walk back to the machine, scouring the store from her vantage point, searching for some evidence that she had landed in the correct year and century. Everything looked as it had when she left, except that now the lights in the front of the store were being turned off, and Tressa realized that the handful of people who still remained in the store were in the process of gathering their things. Tressa rounded the corner and found the humble looking microfilm machine, shut off again, with her purse, sweater, trench coat, clogs, and the Calvino book all tucked neatly underneath the desk below. Tressa hurriedly slipped into her clogs, grabbed her sweater and coat without putting them on, and was about to swing her handbag onto her shoulder when she remembered the article she had printed out earlier that day. She rooted around in her bag and pulled it out, flipping through it quickly, not sure of what she was looking for. She found it on the last page with the date of the article next to the author's name.

May 2013.

Tressa did not feel she really needed any confirmation about all that had transpired within the space of that day, but she still felt a certain sense of validation, nonetheless, that she was holding an article that would not be published for close to a decade and a half later. She tucked the article inside the book, and as she started to walk away, Tressa noticed the reservation pod sitting there next to that oracular machine, now looking innocuous with its dark screen. Tressa contemplated tapping the pod to see if it would reveal anything else, but decided the best thing would be to return it to the front desk.

When she got there, the owner in the leather vest was busy turning off the various coffee machines, as well as the remaining lights in that quadrant of the store. When he saw Tressa, he flashed her a wry, ambiguous smile and asked if she had found everything she needed.

Tressa hesitated for a moment, and then shrugged off the possible double entendre of his statement as she pushed the reservation pod in his direction.

"Yes, thank you. I wanted to return this. I took it earlier when I was waiting for a computer, and then forgot all about it."

The man's smile faded and he passed the pod back across the counter, tapping Tressa on the knuckles to emphasize his next message:

"Keep it. You never know when you might need it again. If nothing else, it can serve as a souvenir…"

Tressa could not summon the energy to question the man's intentions further, so she simply thanked him and slipped the pod into her purse. Seeing that the front of the store was dark, she decided to head out the back door instead.

"Miss – you don't want to go out that way."

"I'm sorry, why not?"

"The fire alarm. It will go off as soon as you open the door, and it's wired to notify the local fire department. I'd like to ring in the new millennium without that kind of excitement if I can avoid it…"

Tressa laughed nervously, wondering if she should pump this man for some information. What was he, some kind of gatekeeper? He obviously knew something. Did other people come to this store with the express purpose of initiating one of these journeys? Were there other gatekeepers like Loren, the photographer that Ellis knew? She should have thought to ask Ellis that question.

Whether it was her fatigue, the mature Ellis's distillation of the various quantum theories of parallel realities, or the sensation of serenity and contentment that inexplicably washed over her in that moment, Tressa decided to let it all go.

"Happy New Year!"

Tressa uttered this with an almost inebriated lilt in her voice. She then started to grope her way through the virtual darkness, bumping into the occasional bookshelf in the overcrowded store, wondering why the owner could not have managed to illuminate even a ribbon of the corridor between the café counter and the front door. At that moment, a patch of florescent bulbs flashed on above her head, buzzing to hearken their arrival.

"Hey! Happy New Year, New Century, and New Millennium to you, my dear!"

Tressa looked back as the man called this out to her, just in time to see him salute her with his fingers on the top of his bare head, an odd gesture that resembled a man in a Charlie Chaplin movie tipping his hat to a passing woman.

Tressa pulled open the front door. It was now completely dark outside. The rain had stopped, but it had become even colder and she paused to slip into her sweater and cinch her trench coat tight. She guessed it was only shortly after six, but New Year's revelers were already out in the streets. Some were dressed elegantly, obviously on their way to parties, or to restaurants offering fixed New Year's deals that promised hors d'oeuvres, prime rib, dessert, entertainment, and a glass of champagne, for one hyper-inflated price.

In that moment, Tressa felt an aching and realized that she missed Daniel terribly. She missed Kassie too, and of course Ellis, but she was filled with an urgent desire to get back to Daniel and pour her heart and soul into the craterous cracks that had formed in their marriage. She no longer cared about what he had done, or said, or what she had felt, or contemplated. Whose fault it all was, ultimately, was completely irrelevant to her. All she knew in that moment was that she wanted Daniel by her side, holding her hand, calling her *baby* as he used to not that long ago. On her way to a public phone, Tressa passed a young couple in paper hats with Y2K written in gold glitter, sneaking swigs of something in a brown paper bag. She rooted around in her open purse for her phone card, but remembering her city smarts at the last moment, zipped up her bag and held it tight against her body. Instead, she placed a collect call to Daniel, holding her breath, hoping that he would be home, and that he would be at least moderately happy to hear from her.

No sooner had Daniel accepted the charges from the operator that he almost shrieked,

"Oh my God, Tressa! What's happened?"

"Nothing, darling. I just wanted to tell you that I am very sorry we are not spending this night together and..."

Tressa's voice quavered slightly as she choked out the next four words, tears collecting in her eyes.

"I miss you terribly."

There was a protracted pause on the other end of the line and Tressa anticipated that Daniel's next words would be something like, *Tressa, we need to talk...* or, *Tressa, there's something I need to tell you...*

Instead, she heard him laugh; it sounded like a laugh of relief. Then he exclaimed, with all the sincerity and emotion she knew he could muster,

"I miss you too, *baby*. Terribly. I can't wait to have you back tomorrow."

"Happy New Year, my love. Kiss Kassie for me, and tell her I can't wait to see her."

Tressa hung up the phone and decided to make her way to a taxi stand she had seen on her first trip to the bookstore with Regina. On her way, she passed

everal bars that were already in full swing. One bar, the "Europa," was decorated in
he spirit of everything eighties. Its name was spelled out in hues of neon pink and
reen, and framed Warhol-esque montages of Madonna, Prince, and David Bowie
dorned the walls. Tressa stopped near the door, catching snatches from an eighties
ribute band that was surprisingly good. Feeling light and somewhat giddy, Tressa
ollowed a group of new arrivals inside the Europa and made her way to the bar.
he ordered a glass of champagne, swiveled around to face the band, and set her
oat and purse on the stool next to her. The lead singer encouraged his audience to
oin in if they knew the next tune, "Under the Milky Way" by The Church. Tressa
lid not recognize the song, but its haunting melody and moody lyrics felt like the
erfect accompaniment to what she had just been through. She sipped her
hampagne and cautiously swayed her upper body in time to the music.

The roar of the crowd joining in on the refrain drowned out the gentle
ums and vibrations steadily emanating from the now forgotten device, its red lights
lashing, inside Tressa's purse.

ABOUT THE AUTHOR

Pia L. Bertucci was born and raised in Chicago, Illinois. At the age of 24, she moved to Chapel Hill, North Carolina to attend Graduate School at The University of North Carolina, where she received a Ph.D. in Romance Languages, with a specialization in Italian. She is currently the Director of the Italian Program at The University of South Carolina in Columbia, where her teaching and research interests include Southern Italian Writers and Italian Food Culture.

Made in the USA
San Bernardino, CA
10 February 2016